Advance Praise for

AN IMPOSSIBILITY OF CROWS

"A text of baleful beauty, like its monster, this book is somehow both achingly tender and ruthlessly unsentimental—and about the most sentimentalised aspects of our sadistic culture, too."

—CHINA MIÉVILLE, author of *Perdido Street Station*

"*An Impossibility of Crows* is a mesmerizing and wholly original novel that scratched an itch I didn't even know I had. Ominous, profound, and compulsively readable, a Gothic novel written in crystalline prose. A flat-out knockout."

—LAURA LIPPMAN, *New York Times* bestselling author

"*An Impossibility of Crows* is, itself, impossibly lyric and ambitious, an Iliad of parenting, of ambivalence, self-sacrifice, and care. A divorce-poem and a tale of scientific obsession—tragic, feminist, and sublime as Shelley's Frankenstein, but quick-paced, wry and gorgeous for the 21st century."

—JORDY ROSENBERG, author of *Confessions of the Fox* and *Night Night Fawn*

"This book is an intensely moving exploration of the way we risk everything we have for the ones we love and still get it wrong. Agnes and Solo will power my heart for a long time. Every sentence of this novel gives more than I thought possible."

—JAC JEMC, author of *Empty Theatre* and *The Grip of It*

AN IMPOSSIBILITY OF CROWS

AN IMPOSSIBILITY OF CROWS

KIRSTEN KASCHOCK

UNIVERSITY OF MASSACHUSETTS PRESS
Amherst and Boston

Printed in the United States of America

ISBN 978-1-62534-925-5 (paper)

Designed by Jen Jackowitz
Set in FreightText Pro
Printed and bound by Books International, Inc.

Cover design by adam b. bohannon
Cover art (detail) by Kawanabe Kyosai, *Crow Flying in the Snow*, c. 1887.
(MET, 14.76.61.34). Courtesy Charles Stewart Smith Collection.
Gift of Mrs. Charles Stewart Smith, Charles Stewart Smith Jr., and
Howard Caswell Smith, in memory of Charles Stewart Smith, 1914, CC0 1.0.

Library of Congress Cataloging-in-Publication Data

Names: Kaschock, Kirsten author
Title: An impossibility of crows / Kirsten Kaschock.
Description: Amherst : University of Massachusetts Press, 2026. |
Series: Juniper Prize for Fiction |
Identifiers: LCCN 2025027240 (print) | LCCN 2025027241 (ebook) |
ISBN 9781625349255 paperback | ISBN 9781685752088 ebook |
ISBN 9781685752095 epub
Subjects: LCGFT: Fiction | Novels
Classification: LCC PS3611.A785 I47 2026 (print) | LCC PS3611.A785 (ebook)
LC record available at https://lccn.loc.gov/2025027240
LC ebook record available at https://lccn.loc.gov/2025027241

British Library Cataloguing-in-Publication Data
A catalog record for this book is available from the British Library.

The authorized representative in the EU for
product safety and compliance is Mare-Nostrum Group.
Email: gpsr@mare-nostrum.co.uk
Physical address: Mare-Nostrum Group B.V.,
Mauritskade 21D, 1091 GC Amsterdam, The Netherlands

For my mother, her sister(s), my sisters, their mothers

Contents

AN IMPOSSIBILITY OF CROWS

The crows like to insist a single crow is enough to destroy heaven. This is incontestably true, but it says nothing about heaven, because heaven is just another way of saying: the impossibility of crows.

–F. Kafka

v

A peeling white barn with starry hex sign
two backroad hours from elsewhere.

A crow inside, the size of a horse.

Wallace Stevens does not number this
predicament among his thirteen ways. Yes

—one knows some poetry.

V

AUG29

Solo I bred for my daughter Mina. I thought I'd give her wings, and now . . . now I'm not sure what I was thinking.

Bruce has just this week filed for divorce. I got papers.

After my dad died old (he had me old) and of hatred, I returned to our farm in Letort. My husband and daughter came with. There were questions.

I can't blame Bruce—if I were him, I would've left me. But he took Mina with him. Of course he did.

I still have questions. Would Solo have let Mina ride him? Given his mass, will he be able to lift himself into the air at all? And if yes, will he want to be flown? To be ridden with girlhood? God knows I never wanted that. But can a bird be said to want anything? Can a girl?

Questions persist.

I'm no biologist. I was a chemist, before. But this is all new to me, a new way of thinking. Crows are never inert. They're labile, reactive—they shift. Except their eyes.

Their eyes are maybe a little bit dead.

Bruce and Mina left in winter. This spring came and went like a sad song. It's almost September. I've been spending a good deal of time alone with the crow. It's been a summer of Solo. Solo and summer and me, the barn like an oven. Me and my black bird baked in a pie.

Solo hot. He says.

Yes, I say.

I have, of late, been finding it advisable to respond to my experiment.

Solo is a fantastic mimic. Most Corvidae are. That's Latin for smart, loud birds like ravens, magpies, jays, and nutcrackers. Bruce once called me *nutcracker*, a joke made after the ballet.

Mina was maybe two that year. We still lived in the city. It wouldn't snow.

Once Solo started talking, I had to name him. He and I are both "solo." Also a joke. I am, in fact, very low. So low. That much should be obvious.

I've tried to educate the bird, but he resists.

I seem to have that effect on my charges. Bruce might say it's because I call them charges but Bruce is gone, was leaving even before he left. Before he took Mina away.

I've decided to start keeping a sort of diary. Ruth kept one—I didn't know. I found a leather folio up in the attic last week among everything Pop boxed up when she died. Her annotating script, meticulously small. Blue.

I opened it. I shut it.

I built the crow for Mina. To my knowledge, this success has no precedent, but I've been lax. I need to make a record. There are so many bits to collect, weave together.

I do feel compelled to say (should this journal one day prove of interest) that these pages are liable to be more musing than lab note, as I am no longer a scientist.

I finished with that when it finished with me.

These days? I don't know what I am. I'm shit with people and I'm shit without. It's only with Solo I'm good.

Or, not good, but home.

∨

Hatching calculus:
all you might have been finds
its limit in what you are.

~BN

Chapter One
AN EXPERIENCE OF CROWS

V

SEPT12

Returned from a walk early this morning, the dawn—saccharine-pink. I'm not sleeping well.

Solo asks: *Solo fly?*

I ignore him for a while. A long while. He starts digging. There is a long trough in the stable, a dry moat of Solo's frustration.

Stop that, I tell him.

Why stop?

It's annoying, I say.

Answering questions is part of the project: how smart is he? is he learning? how much? I'm at the desk in the corner, boiling coffee water on the hotplate.

Why Agnes drink?

Why Solo drink? I fire back.

Last week I read a study on the use of mirroring to establish rapport with the semi-verbal.

Chapter One

Also I have a hangover.

Solo's chained. An alternative to clipping his wings. One day I'll be able to saddle him. When I'm able to sleep I have dreams about it—mounting a shadow.

A few weeks before he left, Bruce asked me how I could be so selfish. I think he was just hating the house.

It's that kind of house—a quarter mile off the road, falling-down porch, drafty clapboard, impossible for him to keep clean. Who knew the three of us had so much skin? That dust could be spiteful?

According to him, my work was hurting all of us. He insisted that we hadn't sacrificed—uprooting ourselves to relocate to this podunk outpost—only for me succumb to some narcissistic fit.

Asshole prick. Also—love of my life.

I am conflicted.

Solo needs fed. This morning there was a cat out by the pond—easy to catch, trusting, more pettish than a true farm cat should be. A tabby.

We usually do dead things, me and Solo, but I'm feeling generous.

Omnivores on occasion appreciate the thrill of a kill. Just look at all the hunters around here, tiptoeing through the scrub like new fathers, their stupid orange vests announcing intent.

I suppose killing does help them stay sharper than not-killing. Though I wouldn't call it sharp exactly, what they are around here.

It doesn't take Solo long.

Birds don't tend to play with their food.

V

A SYMBOLOGY OF CROWS

–from a Himmelsbrief first copied by Aldous Thode @1721, reprinted from the 1855 *Dictionary of Powwowism* with Oma's notes [. . .]. *Perhaps deserving of an update. ~RK*

One crow equals a false friend.

Two crows on the sill and the bread will fall flat.

Three crows can be generous [*ex. the infant lives*], or less so [*the mother bleeds out within the week*].

Four crows is termed an amnesty.

A quorum comprises five crows. A thing may commence, if it is neither a barn raising nor a baptism.

Six crows portend a cold winter after a dry fall.

Seven crows will eat the flesh from any dog.

Eight crows can be trusted to carry on a conversation with the alacrity and the fortitude of drunkards.

Nine crows, upon condemning a man to hang himself, give no solace to widow or heir.

Ten Crows is a children's game played with a corncob, a ball of twine, and a long, forked stick above a limestone spring. [*~a divination still indulged in the greater Lancaster area despite several churches' admonishments against*]

Eleven crows could not agree even upon a worm's cause of death.

To bake a proper beating heart, the practicer requires, for the boil, twelve live crows.

Chapter One

⌄

SEPT17

It's raining. When it rains hard like this the roof of the barn gets so I can't think. Tin.

I knew early on not to let Solo's voice get as big as he was going to get.

He can't amplify his caw. I did that for us, a minor surgery. He still makes all sorts of unpleasant sounds. Like now, against the rain.

Grraaaawpph!

Jesus—he screeches like a banshee when he's deeply pissed, but his voice is not much louder than his relatives' of a more usual size.

I don't know when he'll stop growing. Each day he seems to fill the barn a little more.

His mother was as big as a Great Dane. Her daughter grew a bit larger. Her first son looked like he might be the size of a pony, but she tore out his throat before he was done maturing. (Decreased sociability has been an ongoing problem.) I had to remove her, the mother.

So far Solo has been more docile than his predecessors, but Corvids are known for tool use, insight, and planning. It would be unwise to trust him. He's cawing now. Not in the normal series of threes or fours, but ceaselessly. He sounds congested, strangled. Distraught.

What he needs is to understand who's in charge. That it's me. And what that means is I could put him down if necessary.

And the rain? That sounds like gunshots the next block over, but I'm not in the city. Not anymore.

AN EXPERIENCE OF CROWS

V

Before he left, Bruce said I should let *the idea of us* go. But whose idea was that? He won't be coming back. For a while I thought he would, but no. This house isn't a waiting room—it's a withering room. Moving back made sense on paper, but I knew better.

It's been two and a half years since we came in through the side door by way of the fallow kitchen garden. The front porch was rotting, still is. Bruce had Mina on his hip. Pop, my father Ort Krahn, died on that porch not three months before that.

We'd just settled with the company. We needed a new start, but I knew. I knew this place would not tolerate us.

We hung coats and hats on the mudroom pegboard and put our shoes on the low shelf. Bruce and I were both raised in shoeless homes, but that's the end of such similarities. He was an only child, I had a sister. His parents were alive and kind. Mine, not. I noticed the wooden floor was warped and graying below the farm sink and made a note: repair.

Ruth had jags, stretches when she kept this room daily spotless, zealously sweeping the entry back to square one. Essential, my mother said, to start each new day new, to put—every night—each day in its place, to cabinet what could be cabineted, sweep what could be swept. These spells sometimes lasted weeks. Whenever one would start, she'd go buy a new straw mat from Zimmers' Farm Store, always one with the same black tulip design.

What she was wanting was not really newness.

The day we moved in, there was no mat. The last had disintegrated decades before, and Ort's boots had had time to do their damage. A pair of short black waders stood propped against the wall beside the door. They were spattered with dried November mud. I assume November—he'd died in November.

Chapter One

It was February.

Is this our new house? Mina asked.

It's my old house.

Bruce agreed. *It is most definitely old.*

He spoke while maneuvering Mina to his other hip, removing both their coats easily, expertly. The child was light.

He'd only been in town twice before. Those times, for my sister's wedding and Pop's funeral, we'd stayed at a B&B in Lancaster that sported Fourth of July bunting year round. Bruce was wary but the Harleys had been friendly enough. Friendlier than Ort. Sad for us, for his death.

Should we take a look around? he asked.

Mina nodded. They moved as one into the kitchen. I followed.

Why is there a fireplace in a kitchen?

I heard my daughter but didn't answer. On the other side of the house, through the kitchen window, the long-dead locust tree stood, heavy with its black birds.

Bruce jumped in.

So, do we take the grand tour? Or do you want me to get your walker first?

Mina flung her arm out magnanimously.

First, I want to see it all.

No you don't, I thought.

The birds were quiet. That wouldn't last.

My husband and daughter proceeded toward the front of the house. I was the natural guide, but they didn't bother inviting me. They knew by then how to adjust to my sudden absence in a room. They left it.

V

SEPT18

Second day of rain. Solo paces: his feet, somehow both reptilian and machine-like. At the end of scaled toes longer and thicker than my forearms, Solo's talons gouge scars in the barn floor. The black of wrought iron—they are curved railroad spikes. As he circles, he shakes himself occasionally, throwing off some dark thought or parasite, reminding me of hospital Bruce, Mina's early days.

Solo will never father his own brood. Originally, I wanted to husband him to his sister but he wouldn't have it. Not until she died, and then it was of no use.

The ducks in the pond are forceful. A group of them will hold another down, under the water even, "behaving" her. Duck gang rape is an epigenetic quirk. They've been doing it ever since humans have been observing them and more I'd bet, on average, since their domesticated numbers have skewed male. Too many drakes with their strange elongated corkscrew penises. The female's vaginas have adapted in response: they can twist the opposite way.

Some even have forking paths to catch unwanted sperm, blind alleys.

Crows—like most birds who are not ducks—lack external genitalia and mate through what is called a cloacal kiss. This ritual resembles the end of one of the last-call brawls out the window in our Kensington neighborhood, two sloppy drunks batting at each other as they cling together, failing to stay upright.

I wish I could walk Solo over to the mallards at the pond to show him how it's done. But it's raining and if it weren't, they'd flee. His has become an unnatural presence. Ducks are domesticated but not without instinct, not without self-preservation. Without friends, Solo will have to learn to take what he needs.

I do understand his reticence, though. You can't ever truly know what mechanical deceits hide inside a female. In a very physical way, we are liars.

Animals raised in captivity harbor hidden violences—or they exhibit a kind of looping catatonia. The best thing to do is to maintain a stimulating environment for them, but this barn is in no way that. Solo's sister starved herself here. (In humans, such idiocy occurs only in societies where food is abundant, in homes where it is.) Solo made his one primal move when he woke to find her emaciated body on the ground.

I thought he was trying to rouse her, but it was more than that. When he began tearing at her, animating her corpse by aggressively rooting in the abdominal cavity (among other actions), I scared him away with Pop's rifle. This was an odd behavior for a crow but not wholly undocumented. I documented it. Some kind of fight/flight/feed/fuck confusion. I took my notes, then drove him off to rid the barn of what was left of her.

Because he's alone now and has been for some months, it's on me to keep him engaged.

What's wrong, Solo? You tired of the rain?

Why rain?

Like many Corvids, he imitates speech. He understands some, as much as a dog, maybe more. So I give him an answer: Rain is good for the wheat and corn you need—except when it's filled with poison and this rain is. I know the bastards who put it in there.

Why rain?

Clearly this was too much information.

I try again: How's this?—because good.

Bring Solo?

"Bring" is what Solo says when he wants to go outside. Because everything from outside I have to bring in to him. "Bring" is Solo's nickname for anything beyond his immediate vision. When things disappear—out the door, down his gullet, into the dark—he calls them "bring." When he wants to disappear he says, *Bring Solo.*

He's not having a good day.

Next week, Tuesday, would have been Bruce's and my twelfth anniversary. Neither am I.

⌄

SEPT20

Last night a dozen Polaroids fell out of Ruth's diary. On their backs were our ages and names: Agnes and Bethany, Bethany and Agnes.

I remember Ruth behind that camera. Pop hated it but we thought it was magic—instant pictures—though not really. The three-minute up-fade from milky cloud to flesh, that was my sister's favorite part.

We were she said like backwards ghosts.

I retrieved them from the floor, the murky squares. Layers of time, picked off the body of a life. Small thickened moments.

Scabs.

I haven't been able to bring myself to read any of it, Ruth's book. I can only imagine—given the rubbish our mother heaped on us—what rot she kept to herself.

⌄

Our first months in the house Bruce and I had stayed busy. We scrubbed, sanded, and caulked. We hauled away the detritus of Ort: worn coats from the pegboard, expired goods from the pantry, fishing magazines and almanacs—issues running right up until his death. We left his now-ancient desktop hooked up in the dining room, the one I bought for him the day after my dissertation defense. I told Pop my internship-turned-job at DDR paid better than I knew how to spend. Really, I was celebrating my independence: a decade of school during which I'd asked for not a cent.

The behemoth, though temperamental, still fired up. Mina played solitaire while we worked and, when she got tired of that, Bruce showed her a website where she could splatter color across the screen like Jackson Pollock. Clever programming—but Mina needed practice holding a pen. She needed work on her letters.

Can I choose the colors for the rooms?

The girl wanted too much. Her life was not going to be like that.

Off-white, I told her. The rooms are staying the same, we're just brightening them.

Why?

Because we aren't staying long, I explained. Again.

She knew we were fixing up the place to sell. The realtor had said neutral was better and to take advantage of the light, I reminded her. Mina was six, plenty old for reasons.

Then Bruce did the thing he does. Plopped himself down on the cheap couch lugged from Philly because Ort owned nothing soft and smiled a smile designed for her but aimed at me.

*The off-white keeps the light cold. Maybe Mina could pick us out some coffees and caramels to look at? There *are* other neutrals.*

Then he framed his own face, the burnt sienna of certain ferric oxide solutions, with thumbs and first fingers.

No.

I offered nothing more. The house had never really been about reasons. Or warmth. A repository for six generations' distrust of outsiders and otherness, science and self—that's what we were fixing to sell.

V

SEPT21

Something's wrong with Solo. It's not good for him to be alone so much, cut off from his kind. I stay in the barn late, sometimes sleep here. It's no solution.

Midnight, and he's finally out. He's tucked his head along his muscled back and folded his legs under him, though—like a horse—he can and often does sleep standing. This nest-like posture is rarer. I'd say he was exhausted but it could be the opposite . . . he's hardly moved in days. This afternoon he spent an hour eerily immobile, lost in himself, his eyes cast like empty hooks in my direction.

He half-preens in his sleep, dragging his beak sluggishly once or twice through a wing. Maybe some sort of self-soothing behavior? Mina used to suck on her fingers, all four. When I'd go to pull them out, Bruce would stop me. *Let her be, it's not a thing.* I was sure it was, in fact, a thing—another developmental anomaly I'd gifted her with.

Solo just twitched—and I found myself startling. Which is ridiculous since I don't scare . . . not at horror movies, not the news. Bruce claims this is the sign of an empathetic defect, an inability to be moved by others' misfortune. He's been wrong about a few things since I've known him, most of them me.

Last week I downloaded some articles, ethology research rife with bad reasoning and poor conclusions. It's a fuzzy science—if you can call it that—decidedly unlike chemistry. Though a few of the publications show more rigor. It appears that sleeping birds do exhibit REM and neuronal activity. They may dream. The scans comparing their waking and non-waking brain patterns are fairly convincing: songbirds may replay song, for example.

Solo's daily life is less than ideal. It lacks variation, opportunities for socialization. He's bored. His brain, vast for a crow's, is limited by what it encounters. A dream is supposed to act as the mind's scratch pad—a place where deep memory and new experiences can be worked out, consolidated.

This barn may be starving his dreams.

Earlier, when I went up to the house to grab dinner, I heard the evening jabber of crows in the locust. I'm thinking of recording their harangue and playing it for Solo—would the sounds enliven or disquiet him? The birds were the deep bassline of my childhood soundtrack, the farm's white noise, only black. Now they grate on me.

But if Solo benefits, my discomfort is immateri—fuck. He just twitched again.

∨

SEPT24

I leafed through Ruth's mess this morning: loose sheets tucked and other scraps taped in—pictures, typewritten paragraphs, handwritten recipes and passages. I stopped at a page addressed to us. So this was not a diary exactly. Or not simply.

DEAR AGNES, DEAR BETHANY,

> *I know there are questions you will want answered, ones that you haven't been brave enough to ask. This is not what anyone expected, certainly not your father. He assumed he'd go first, I'm guessing, one of the few advantages of marrying someone so very much younger.*

I've read all your misgivings—how could I not?—flickering across your faces as if your faces were candles. And they're like candles, the way they light up and how they get melty when you're confused or sleepy or when I am.

Bethany, it does hurt but no more than I can bear.

Agnes, of course I love him.

This was typical of her. That had never been my question.

∨

SEPT26

Solo's bigger every day. When I come back from the house, he stretches his wings and holds them out as he struts around . . . it's like a boast. He's more erratic too. The crowsound I've introduced to our mornings so far has had mixed results: today he's alternating between irritation and lethargy—I think he may need more space for exercise. He said as much.

Solo bring.

I know, Solo. I know.

Bring I Solo. Bring.

I've been planning next steps, using software to map the optimal timeline for flight. But this is uncharted territory and I get distracted. I learned yesterday, for example, that Bruce has a new publication coming out. It's a chapbook (whatever that is) from a micro-press (and that).

A few weeks ago, I brought my engagement ring out to the barn to show Solo—crows do in fact like the shiny—it's a fake peacock sapphire in an art deco setting, a ring that satisfied my husband's need for symbols without bankrupting us *monetarily or morally*. But it was too big, too showy. I couldn't wear it to work, not under latex. Recently I've been putting it on to write. I know it's silly . . . but it makes me feel like it's not yet defunct. My life.

Occasionally I scan Bruce's social media for mentions of Mina. Why shouldn't I? She's mine too. He's had her call me a few times since they left, the last back in August. His parents, the aptly named Nobles, took her sailing on the Chesapeake. He was embarrassed by their largesse—his childhood was over before either had made partner in the firm. It took far longer than it should've he said. For all the reasons, all the isms.

Mina told me how much she liked being out on the water: *So Much.* It bodes well, I suppose. Her fearlessness.

That is, if the next phase goes as it should and Solo proves as trainable as he is smart. I'm not naïve enough to think the one trait guarantees the other. Learning and memory tend to be more highly developed in wild specimens than in birds raised in captivity. But I am committed, and his intellect—undeniable. Still . . . I'll need to plan this carefully.

He's getting so big.

∨

A: Bruce?

B: I'm calling about the papers. Have you signed them?

A: Why would I do that?

B: Ness, we've talked about this. Your daughter and I need to move on.

A: Please put Mina on the phone.

B: (muffled) Mina, it's your mom.

. . .

M: Mom?

A: Mina, hi. How are you? How's Baltimore?

M: It's good. I'm going to school.

A: What kind of school?

M: A regular school. It's big.

A: How are the teachers treating you?

M: Like I'm regular. I have an aide. Linda. She helps me change classes.

A: An aide?

M: You wouldn't like her. She talks too much. But she's funny and she brings me peanut brittle because she says I'm a sweet little nut. Did you know Linda means pretty in Brazilian?

A: Portuguese. Is she pretty?

M: She's old, Mom.

A: Old?

M: Like, your age.

∨

SEPT28

Solo woke up skittish. He's been pacing for hours, his rhythms uneven. I had to unchain him, the shackle chafing his tarsometatarsus. That was a dance on my part, navigating his shifting talons. I tried a recording but it only agitated him. I've been alternating between two separate ten-minute clips of the roost—I may need to make more.

He's been walking the same circuit over and over, looping. I'm not sure he realizes I took him off the chain. I'll need to do some more research on his anxiety if I hope to treat it. I do know it's nearly time for fledging, a precarious time for any bird.

Chapter One

Corvids are extremely familial animals: siblings sometimes return to the nest to help raise younger brothers and sisters. This is not an option for us. I've been scouting scientific articles for alternatives, and gleaning what I can from history, fiction even. Old books offer a ton of insight so long as I can separate fact from fantasy. Novelists are the worst, but they offer the thickest description.

He squawks at me—if I've been reading too long.

All sorts of writers have had Corvid fixations: that keeps coming up. Lord Byron kept a menagerie that included peacocks and a tame bear along with a crow. Poe famously wrote about the vocal talents of a raven. Dickens kept a pet raven named Grip. Truman Capote called his crow Lola. But it was a Russian writer, Gorky, who to my mind best understood the species: *Once there was a crow, it flew from the field to the hill, from hedge to hedge, and lived its life. Then it died and rotted away. What's the sense in it? There just isn't any!*

No melodrama. Just the routine chaos of the world.

Last fall, Bruce read a bunch of crow poems aloud to me in bed, a book by some man-poet famous for his suicided wife. This was how my husband thought to support my work.

Science fascinates Bruce, though the methods trouble him. There's some deep-seated distrust there. When I've called him on it, he recites this litany:

Unit 731, Tuskegee
Kligman, Sims, and Mengele
Trovan, Depo-provera
Manhattan, MK Ultra

It's from one of his poems, "Proper Nouns and How to Use Them." Of the two of us—he may be the darker.

When I first started with the birds, their clipped wings upset him, their caws. We argued. I told him his qualms weren't ethically compatible: you can't wish someone freedom without wanting them to have a voice.

These aren't someones, Ness.

Solo's great grand-dam and her brothers were the only three of my crows my husband met, and that was before they got to be shepherd-sized and the matriarch plucked out her brothers' eyes.

When I told him she did that, Bruce suggested we head back to the city.

Mina had already boycotted the barn. Bruce was being histrionic, but I didn't bring him out to see the birds again. That was fine with him. He never shared his own work until he was ready to send a manuscript to publishers. Seems I have an incisive mind and an even sharper tongue. My husband has written some excellent poems but tends toward the self-indulgent. To be fair, it's a danger of the trade.

So I stopped bringing up my experiments. We talked daughter instead, an inexhaustible topic. Sometime early last winter, Bruce told me Mina didn't want to do her exercises, she was acting sullen.

She's nine, I said.

Eight. She won't be nine until June.

He shook his head at my lapse—not in disbelief, though. I was always failing in some basic way.

So cabin fever?

*No, but maybe avian flu? . . . I hear *that* can wreak serious havoc.*

Then he chuckled—he finds his own black humor hilarious. I didn't get it. I mean, other than that he was projecting his own static onto Mina. He'd admitted the online classes he was teaching felt sterile, and his recent poems claustrophobic. But I knew he wasn't writing any. The only person who'd ever made art in that house was Ruth. And she'd left no room for other minds.

Bruce had imagined our time here as therapeutic, a way for us to get whole. By which he meant me. But he'd lost patience with my moods and the crows, or vice versa. Whatever. Bruce wanted me to heal, yes, but there was no way our daughter would be a step in my recovery.

When I first decided to raise them, I thought I'd have the crows imprint on Mina. Only that would've required my daughter to join me, and Mina hated the barn. It smelled she said—like sadness.

As if the world needs another fucking poet.

After Pop died, the DDR settlement made it possible to come deal with the farm. It was Bruce who suggested the move. The plan had a certain logic to it: a writing retreat for my long-suffering husband combined with family therapy. And the birds? At first he thought they were some strange kind of grief performance.

> *You know, in some cultures crows are considered messengers—between the living and the dead.*

I asked him not to insult our intelligence.

> *Human intelligence?*
>
> Not human intelligence. Yours, mine.

Bruce didn't love the crow poems he read me—they made him laugh. I didn't like them either, but I don't know that I found them funny. The poet liked to speak of "Woman" and "Crow" as mythic categories. I think "Crow" stood for the poet himself. But "Woman" clearly meant women, all of them.

Crows may not have personalities, not true sentience, but each one is an individual. *A someone.* One might think they have this trait in common with women. Maybe not.

After he finished that book, we didn't start another together. I began heading up to the attic after Mina was in bed to find other reading material. Sometimes I'd get caught up, not coming down until Bruce was inside a dream, twitching and mumbling.

Once I passed out up there reading a falling-apart 1820 grimoire, John George Hoffman's *Long Lost Friend.* Anti-scientific claptrap—boiled rabbit brains on toothaches, rhymes and saints prescribed for pain. I woke when Bruce yelled out, *Insufficient black! Delete!* I raced down the steps and shook him from the nightmare. He asked if I'd heard the sirens. I told him we weren't in the city anymore, we were safe.

Even though he was still sweating, his heart racing, he laughed at that. Hard.

He'd been stopped twice by local cops our first weeks here. One gave him no reason. The other told him if he's driving the speed limit on a farm road, chances are he's high. *So, you high?*

> What—thought he'd caught a blazing Blasian?
>
> *Go to hell, Ness.*

I know a thousand ways to fail.

Unlatching him seems to have cheered Solo. While I've been writing, he's stopped walking that same floor pattern. What he's doing now looks more like a dance . . . two hops forward, one zig back. Three zags forward, five hops back. It's mesmerizing—an algorithmic tango. Incantatory bop.

v

A crow bereft of
f/light consumes
her own.

~BN

Chapter Two

A LIBRARY OF CROWS

∨

Oct3

I've been talking out loud to the bird. I think this may be good for him (better at least than the crow tapes he asks for) but not necessarily for me. Last night I headed out to Junco's.

I was alone at the bar when a hulk of a man came in from another bar and fumbled himself onto the stool beside me.

Anyone here?

Nope, I said. No one in the world.

World's a shithole.

Great, a philosopher. But I'd showed up hoping for conversation and this was what I'd been given. He was right—a shithole.

You think? I asked him.

I know it.

How do you?

I been waking up every goddamned morning without Maisie.

Divorced. That, or a widower—you fucking kidding me? But I was two drinks in myself, committed.

Your wife?

He didn't answer immediately. He ordered a beer for crying into. Once he was sure it was on its way, he started in.

Maisie was the best Labrador ever swum in Cocalico Creek.

An unexpected turn.

I'm sorry, I said.

But I wasn't, not really.

Eleven years old. Too goddamned young. Hips, arthritis—got bad quick. Had to put her down Tuesday. Wife's a bitch but Maisie, Maisie was the best goddamned bitch a man could have.

I wanted to laugh but thought he'd take it the wrong way. Instead I ordered another whiskey and soon we were chatting like half-brothers. No names, but we hugged at the end of the night, patting each other's backs too many times, my face in his chest, my arms barely reaching around the hot-cider barrel of him. He smelled like diesel. We told each other to be careful getting home and I somehow managed.

When I woke up dry-mouthed in the barn, Solo ignored me, like I'm some goddamned disappointment. So I headed back up to the house.

Chapter Two

⌄

Daughters,

Today I watched you two playing cards together, cross-legged on the floor—Go Fish, if I'm not mistaken. The thing about Go Fish is you have to be honest about what you have in your hand or it's pointless, but there you were, taking turns lying to each other.

I can only write on my good days, and they're getting fewer. I feel it, I feel it in my chest and my throat and my stomach, I feel it in my teeth, in my jaw, in my shoulder blades and in my shins. This is what it must feel like inside a seed, the container failing what it contains. I suppose mothers are a kind of seed, no? Destroyed as they produce, no real trace of them in the flower.

Vessel-dom isn't really something to be proud of, is it? I carried you into the world, me a jar and you the ink. Then you spilt out of me, leaving me invisible again and somehow more fragile.

This is why I prefer you call me Ruth.

I wonder if you'll carry forward any of me, in stain or shard. I hope not. You should be all your own, bloom not hue, more daisy than dye. Do you remember when we fed ink to the Queen Anne's lace and it turned the color of sky? Remember later when you learned the same plant, unyanked, would become a wild carrot? When it finally wilted, you were sad, the both of you, and you asked me why it was dying, and I told you: Silly girls! because we brought it into the house.

I need to be clear about my mother—she was never honest about her hand. I think she often forgot she was supposed to be holding anything at all.

V

OCT4

Solo is unhappy with me.

I'm beginning to worry that my isolation is causing me to anthropomorphize the bird. Scientists working with model systems (~animals) talk about this often. There were rat and mice people at DDR. They tested chemicals in these lesser mammals, mostly to screen for lethality (~death) before we moved the drugs into clinical or atmospheric trials (~on humans/~airborne).

One of the mouse lab technicians, Soren, and I were friendly. This was before. We were the only two smokers in our wing of the building and often met on the roof above the cafeteria where our colleagues couldn't throw their dirty looks.

We talked. Soren missed the endless light of summer days in Kuopio. I knew nothing of them. He described the sky of his childhood and the lakes surrounding his small city. He described his family home: simple, furnished in warm wood, nearly silent. The silence—this was why he left. I spoke less than he did, which maybe reminded him of home, and only about work. I asked about his mice.

> *They have souls*, he told me.
>
> You can't believe that.
>
> *Do you believe the world is mostly in darkness?*

It was a strange thing to ask, but I didn't have friendships with normal people. Soren and I were knowingly colluding on two separate, slow-motion suicides. We laughed about it. We laughed often—if only about death and only our own. So I was honest. Yes, I said, almost entirely in.

> *So I torture and kill mice for a living. I am just part of the dark waltz.*

Maybe he listened to too much metal, but I had no trouble thinking of Soren as a murderer. Or as a poet. Hell, Bruce was one. Bruce actually called himself a failed poet, but I don't think you can fail at a profession that refuses to ascribe any metric for success.

It was Soren's decision to confess I found strange. He claimed to be an atheist. I challenged him. What do they do to show you their souls?

They learn. They fear. They love.

Love?

They love me, their executioner.

That was all he said. His hand shook a bit, but it sometimes did. I was married. Bruce and I were a few years in, enough that I assumed he must have realized his mistake, that it was only his doggedness keeping us together. Bruce pestered me to quit, so I smoked more at work than at home. I knew Soren's hands.

Soren and I, a few weeks after this conversation, made love on that roof, in a little gulf between two access staircases. It happened once, it was uncomfortable—physically because of the tarpaper and for other reasons we did not discuss. I assume he was given to remorse. Because of the mice. We never mentioned the transgression and never repeated it. A few months later I found I was pregnant, and he returned to graduate school in Finland.

Mina could not have been his, but that has always seemed entirely beside the point.

∨

B: Hello.

A: Bruce.

B: What is it? Is something wrong?

A: Happy anniversary.

B: Jesus, Ness.

v

Oct6

Solo reminded me of Mina today. He scratched at the wall with his beak, sharpening it, ignoring me. He didn't eat what I gave him, not even the live mice I catch with the sticky traps. There were two new from last night. Too minor a meal for the work they would take, I guess. That—or he was being petulant. When he wouldn't do it, I had to put them out of their misery.

Solo watched me kill them. As I did it, he opened wide as if waiting for me to toss in the small carcasses, but then reconsidered and snapped what seemed his whole throat shut. I used a hammer because their heads weren't free to twist—to snap the necks. And because of the hammer I had to clean up after. That's when Solo pressed me.

Agnes eat.

I don't eat mice, Solo.

Agnes eat.

I hadn't eaten all day, it was true, but his concern for me can be so childish and so fucking repetitive.

I went up to the house and made myself some soup. Campbell's vegetable beef and barley. As I ate, I flipped through Ruth's book. She'd made a strange sort of confession—laced with evidence against her, with testimonials.

Chapter Two

V

*Workings of Sky and Earth**

I shall not weep, not sadden my Lord.
To ask his mercye, my only word.
My tears will not know crow, nor corn, nor moon.
My hands onlie earth, my heart Christ's wounds.

~

Where the stream flows, we follow it back. We unburden ourselves, until we are like children in the garden, seeking our source, seeking a spring where we myght drink without fear. O temperance. O patience. O lamb and rabbit. O hen and doe. O proud black bird. O fish frivolous ~ how we pity you, carried along the current, no hands to work the soil, to grasp the roote, having not the strength to leap up the tumbled rocks, to batter your scales in pursuit of a just and loving God.

~

Where our dear sister has gone
The birds await their shaping songs.
When our blue sister now sings
Notes drip His reign upon their wings.

~

Acts filled with requirement are rightly called Prayers.
When at odds with necessity, any act becomes surfeit ~ a sin.
Gluttony is an error in bodily judgment ~ Greed and Lust are species of Gluttony.
The body does not need conjugation with power, nor possession, nor any other body, nor even the upper rooms of the air, being Utter.

Pride is an error in estimation of that Utterness.
Envy is an error in estimation of that Utterness in others.
Sloth is to fear right action, and Wrath to act beyond righteousness ~ the flight into God must come by Faith alone.
Hew to what is essential and be delivered from excess. First, pluck the Black. Then whet the soul's knife ~ to shear from itself ~ befouling flesh.

**Fragments from a brief organization of seventeenth-century celibate believers called the Cistern. In 1882, forty-two documents written on scraps of fabric were found in a Bible under a floorboard in their Great House, now an abandoned mill on a fishless creek. These passages I copied from a handsewn copy of those pieces presented to Hannah Krahn (Oma) along with* The Sixth and Seventh Books of Moses *on the day of her wedding, in 1928. ~RK*

∨

OCT7

I went up to the attic today, in daylight. Pop's bed is there, cot really, a walnut dresser with lamp, an empty rolling clothes rack made of pipe, a reading chair. Together, these frame out a bedroom on the north end by the small back window.

On either side, thin walls drop down from a sloped, dormer-less roof, hiding storage space and insulation behind access panels, each with a circular metal pull.

At the far end, the front of the house, a large three-sectioned window floods the space with sun. An empty wooden easel stands a few feet back. Beneath that, a Persian carpet—the only thing like it in the house—still retains a kind of imported grace. If Ruth ever used this easel, she rolled the rug back: it's faded, but otherwise pristine.

Chapter Two

I would've set up on this side, for the light. Pop chose the grimmer north.

Nights, the big window is perfect for moon watching, or would've been. If Bethany and I'd been allowed up here. If we'd had a telescope. If Pop had been the sort of person who looked to the sky for something other than guessing at rain—how much will come, how long it's likely to last.

We were not allowed, and we never argued. After Ruth bought an old copy at our library's make-way sale, she read Anne Frank's diary to us. She asked us what we thought the librarian would try to replace it with. Bethany suggested a book with pictures. I made fun of my sister's babyishness, but I had no idea what Ruth was asking of us. The *Left Behind* series was popular at the time.

Attics were unlucky: forgotten spaces where forgotten girls turned into cutouts of themselves. That's how I'd imagined the diary as Ruth read it, as a string of days written onto paper dolls strung across a silent room. Sewn-together stars. She tried her best to explain the Holocaust, but it was impossible to fathom—not the mechanistic, bureaucratic horror—not that. The numbers. How were there so many, and then . . . not? An attic could easily swallow a girl. But what had the stomach for an entire people? I asked Ruth. She answered with no hesitation. *This place.*

Our house? The land beneath it? I imagined quicksand and sinkholes making our fields into a hive of hidden cells lying in wait for a reverse rapture.

When a mind is as literal as mine is, Ruth said it gives words bodies. I never felt that. Bodies were the least real of all the things I knew. To think too much about them was to beg shame, so I didn't. Or—I did. Then, after, tried to will *did* into *didn't*.

Three homemade shelves sag with the weight of her books and boxes and jars on either side of the big window, six total. Pop kept her with him but not with him. The shelves are shaggy with dust and cobwebs, deserted knowledge, secret stacks in a house that was built without the thought of any but a single book. That one is up here too: an immense German Bible inscribed with births and deaths going back to the old country. It sits closed on a wooden pedestal built to bear it. The first birth recorded: Willem Krahn, born 1609, who married Isolde (geborene Thaler) in 1627 and begat seven sons, five of whom made it to adulthood: Willem, ~~Tobias~~, Ortho, Joseph, Samuel, ~~Kilian~~, Basil. No daughters.

In a medical museum Bruce and I visited on a whim a few years back, a progression of large slides hung on a rack, the type of contraption used to display posters or carpet samples. Each slide held a coronal section of a human body sliced so thin it was translucent. I spent an hour paging through a person, wondering what chemicals they'd used to fix the cells. Bruce had been disgusted. By the exhibit first—and then by me.

It didn't stop him from writing a poem about my heartlessness. He read it to me proudly a few weeks later, as if I would not recognize myself in the tinman he had rusting between frames.

I was supposed to go through the attic our first summer here to clear it out but got distracted. Or maybe I didn't want to learn about Ruth that way. Parsed out in layers that would help me understand or, worse, forgive her—trapped as she'd been in someone else's medium.

There was something wrong with my mother—beyond her having married my father.

I may have known this before.

A number of graph papers are folded and tucked between the pages of her diary. I pull them out. Each is filled with a single word repeated hundreds of times in her tight blue script.

Chapter Two

blue

bile

livre

lied

liebe

bride

blood

bird

thread

I spread the pages out. The effect is odd. The words look like wallpaper. The letters run together until I see *able* on the *blue* page. *Bride dribbles* across its sheet like an infant.

Thread becomes *dearth* becomes *breath* becomes *hatred.*

Livre is French for *book*. But no book is free (*libre*).

Liebe—I ~~beliebe~~ believe—is German for *love*. And *lied*, a song without truth.

Bird, spoken aloud one hundred times in a row, sounds a little like *buried*.

Oct10

I went to make coffee in the kitchen this morning. I couldn't. There's a smell. Hard to identify . . . dead animal in the chimney? Whatever it is, it's putrid and it permeates the room. I gagged over the sink but I don't want to call anyone. After months alone, the thought of interaction with a stranger is anxiety-producing—it requires prep, always has.

Doubtless this is why I never dated, not really. Between arriving at college at seventeen and Bruce, I'd slept with two lab partners and initiated maybe a half-dozen awkward hookups in South Philly bars far from campus. They too could stink. I never sought intimacy, never thought it would come. Bruce was a fluke—I knew we wouldn't last. And Mina, Mina was something else entirely.

I poured out a shot and left for the barn.

It was past time for Solo to bathe. I filled the plastic pool we use about halfway up, but when I led him out of his stall, he rooted himself. To get him to follow me, I generally reach up to stroke his breast feathers while talking gently to him. This morning I was babbling about the leaves starting to change outside: how the yellows are well in but the red is still a few weeks out, how the elms will drop their crackling brown with no ceremony—inane shit like that. He did come out, haltingly, into the center of the barn. But he stopped dead a few yards from the green tub I'd set beside the central drain. He stopped and he squawked. Loudly.

What is it Solo?

Red.

I looked around, but I didn't see anything red. Certainly no leaves. I sweep out the barn once a week minimum. His world is almost entirely sepia. I thought I'd misheard.

What did you say?

He didn't answer. Instead he leaned over me, blocking my view of anything but him, and made a quick nip at my upper arm—a puppy asking an older dog to play. The result was not playful. His scissoring beak ripped clean through my jacket and the wool sweater underneath. I've got opposing welts working into dark bruise even as I write this. Sore worse than a tetanus shot.

I yelled at him. Actually I didn't yell. It was shriller than that.

What the fuck was that?

The wall of him juddered, and he stepped back and cocked his head at me. It's true I've never raised my voice with him before—not even after his sister. His response was a little plaintive. Explainy.

Red. Bring red.

Had he been trying to, what . . . cut me? It's possible he's recognized the similarity between my anatomy and that of the protein sources I provide him. To grow at the speed he's been growing, he needs a massive amount of feed (grubs and corn and kibble) plus as many carcasses as I can get my hands on. He could be looking for confirmation that I, too, contain blood and muscle and tendon. This was not necessarily malice—it might be simple curiosity.

I was actually red. I mean I am, in fact, bleeding. I got my period last night.

In the 1820s, the naturalist John James Audubon asserted without fact that birds, specifically carrion eaters, don't smell so well. This untested olfactory theory, if you can call it that, took a century and a half to be debunked by a zoology post-doc touring the Antarctic. She dipped tampons in ultra-pungent compounds, strung them behind her boat to mask the scent with water, and still the birds came. It's called experimentation.

Despite my anger, I walked Solo calmly back to the stall before dumping out the pool. If he gets filthy, itchy, if his mites multiply beyond control, he'll have to roll about to dust himself free of them. I won't be grooming him.

Outside the barn, I threw out the shredded Carhartt Bruce bought for me when we'd first moved back here. There's an ancient leather bomber in the attic that suits me better anyhow. Pop said he kept it for tractor days, and Ruth laughed. She told us he'd bought it to impress her after she'd raved about a picture of him wearing one on a motorcycle in Saigon. My mother could be brilliant, her mental connectivity as startling as sun dogs. As illusory. But when I asked Pop about the bomber, he said it wasn't his. Not the jacket he wore in the field (a Goodwill purchase), not the one she thought she remembered, not the motorcycle. According to him, there was no such photograph. He told us our mother trusted dreams and that she shouldn't. Too many doors in dreams.

When I got up to the house, the smell in the kitchen was worse. I went hunting through the cabinets but only succeeded in making myself nauseous. I opened the side door for some fresh air and heard crows fussing on the other side of the house. Sometimes they seem to have learned words, like Solo has, though I'm sure this is a trick of the wind—the recordings never bear out what I think I'm hearing. Tonight the caws sounded like *Lie!* or *Liar!* or maybe *Wire?* or *Why?* But they weren't delivered as questions. The tone is more assholish. They sound like lawyers.

It's been a cold, raw day.

∨

Oct13

I went away. I needed some time to think. To breathe. I may be avoiding a more in-depth search—for a dead possum under the floorboards, a squirrel in the flue. Whatever it is, it can wait. Wait long enough, and decomposition and desiccation will turn the dead thing to dust. Two more weeks, three tops. Maggots are a potential snag but summer's been over.

Chapter Two

I went to visit my sister in Paradise. She's never left home, the area.

She's birthed six. All with names inspired by her nutcake church: Canon, Honor, Prosper, Merit, Serenity, and Forbearance. How this place manages to gather to it and support its many cults is beyond me. They call the littlest girl Forbes, like the money magazine. It's too perfect. My sister is painfully unaware of what she's bought into. Her group would tithe her out of existence if they could, if she had any money whatsoever. Backwoods shitstains.

Bethany and I weren't raised like this. Pop didn't take us to any Sunday thing. He himself smuggled out the work ethic from his Mennonite forbearers—and the severity—but left behind any kindness.

We've seen each other only once since Pop's funeral—when my sister met Mina. The only time. She'd left her own kids home with Tim, said it was too much for them. But Mina didn't seem upset, maybe because I wasn't. I wore black. Bruce dressed our daughter in a spruce-colored jumper, her white-tighted legs dangling beneath. Driving into town, I saw a paunchy man on a shaky ladder, stringing up fat orange-and-blue fifties-style Christmas bulbs to fight the upcoming bleak.

We tend to think color can do things color can't.

When I got to Bethany and Tim's compound (off a dirt road, four outbuildings including a chicken coop and root cellar, plus a pump beside the house, so yes—compound) she was standing outside in a denim housedress. They too still exist.

I said: Hi, sis.

What are you doing here?

Needed a break from work.

She looked confused. *I thought you were done with that.*

I am. But I've been doing my own thing over at Pop's. It's harder than I expected.

She nodded, and her self-cut bob swung out from behind her ears. My sister's hair is wheat-colored, mine nearly black. Her skin like cream, mine more the color of a destroying angel—a local mushroom Ruth long ago taught us to spot by its gray-green tinge and to avoid because of its tendency to kill.

So how're Bruce and Mina enjoying the homestead?

He left me. A few months back.

Bethany's expression said she knew it would happen. I hadn't known. Bruce was the only person to withstand what she used to call my intensity. I suppose, in her view, there was no way that could last.

All sin, all fall short—

Please Bethany, don't.

He take Mina?

Yeah.

She nodded again. Bruce had raised Mina. Slung her across his chest for years, taught her how to get around better than the doctors predicted, stretched hypertonic limbs. Bruce cooked. Gumbo and galbi, scrambled eggs and salad, if salad were cooked. Bruce sang some old lullabies, retooled others: no cradles falling, no blood diamonds. I approved or disapproved. Bruce prepared and made possible. I vetoed. That was my power—which was all the power—also, none of it.

You want to come in?

The girls were doing chores in the house. Honor was minding Forbes—a few weeks old when I'd stopped by last fall to meet her, she was now starting to walk. Walk. They said that, but it looked more like bumping into thing after thing after thing.

The boys Canon and Prosper, I was told, were building a fence to keep loose chickens from wandering out to the main road. Pop taught both his daughters how to build fences, though we hadn't anything to keep in other than ourselves.

Merit sat near us, staring at me intently until her mother sent her to look in on a napping Serenity. She ducked out shyly, but with a sense of importance. Her wild curls flounced—could not pretend shyness, not hide the child's pleasure. I too found doable tasks enjoyable at Merit's age: helping to arrange Ruth's flowers, nabbing nightcrawlers from the compost, brushing out Bethany's hair, longer when we were young. Recently, basic human functions feel impossibly complicated. Maintaining relationships, repairing them.

Bethany made tea.

It was good, comforting, one of her homegrown concoctions: lemon balm, lavender, nettles. We sat without talking for a long while. Our silence was familiar. I'd forgotten how I liked sometimes having it in her presence.

Finally she asked, *This new work, you were saying?*

The farm. Livestock.

Pigs, she said without hesitation. *Do pigs.*

Pigs?

They're smart, eat anything, fetch a good price around here, and some of the Dutch will even trade for waste stuffs, hooves and heads and such. Pigs. Don't know why Pop never.

He hated the living.

She smiled then. Her brightness tamped things down, then cleared them away. It was nothing like Ruth's darker flame. My sister was pale and pretty but our mother had dazzled, even now, glinting through memory's black molasses.

I was thirteen when she died, Bethany eleven.

I don't like pigs, I said. They're fat.

They're supposed to be fat.

I'm raising birds.

Hmm . . . that could work. Emus? I could loan you some hens . . .

No. Crows.

She looked at me the way she'd always looked at me when I wasn't making sense. She'd played Igor when I made fertilizer explosives or poisons to use on the rats because Pop wouldn't bring even a cat into the house after his wife died.

Bethany had a few burn scars, as did I. Mine were worse. I tried to protect her but she couldn't know that because I hadn't been good at it. Ruth hadn't learnt me that particular skill.

I'm breeding crows.

My sister didn't respond.

I helped her fix dinner. Tim was off with his semi. Their farm isn't even subsistence-level and her husband performed only the heaviest labor in the busiest months. She had plenty of hands—what with the children—is what she said he said. I have no clue why she chose him, this life, a second time.

Canon said grace over the spinach and carrots, and then my sister told us all how it was going to be.

Aunt Agnes will be here just until tomorrow morning. She is our guest. You know what God expects of you when we have guests. We are to show our hospitality without grumbling.

Chapter Two

I knew what she was saying. We have a strangled relationship but it wasn't difficult to parse. Barbed wire twisting around a jerking scarecrow. I was in the wind.

I ran away at seventeen. Philadelphia, city of unsisterly love, chemistry scholarship. Bethany stayed with Pop until she met Tim on a market day. She was twenty-eight, Tim was ten years older. He was selling overripe tomatoes at the side of the road for nearly nothing. She bought them for sauce and for feeling sorry. That was the story she told at the wedding five months later. The real story is she got brave somehow. She called me and I came with Bruce, which was awkward: skin still a thing around here, and Bruce brown. It was a sad wedding, sad and nice. Hawaiian Punch and lemonade reception. Greasy scrapple turning paper plates into stained-glass windows.

Then six pregnancies in eleven years, maybe more—I never asked about failures. I came out to see her once every year or two, kid or two. I'd stay an hour to meet whichever sticky new cherub she had swaddled against her. I always drove out alone and without warning. She was never pleased, but what was I interrupting? Bruce suggested my trips were guilt excursions but I don't think I'm capable. Curiosity, more like. Her Honor and my Mina were born the same week. Mina was an accident. That was nine years ago. Our daughters have never met. I can't imagine them meeting in the future.

Bethany could keep going with the kids I guess—I mean having them—but maybe early menopause. Her mustache, though still blonde, is heavier.

After the kids were in their rooms for the night, my sister pointed to the couch. I dropped onto it, suddenly exhausted.

Why crows? she asked, opening a chest in the corner.

I'm breeding bigger ones.

It's not a good idea. Remember Oma.

This was the family lore. Pop's mother was said to have *abilities*: healing, herbalism, augury. She read bird flights for omens and claimed to grasp some language, specifically crow. Ruth told us Oma had learned of her own death from the birds. Pop hated these stories. But Ruth got them from Opa—who lived with them a handful of months before he died—and found them riveting, as did we, when she sat on the edge of our bed recounting them in a voice thick with the unknowable. Folk tripe.

Plus they carry things . . . pestilence.

You know that's not true. They eat pests.

No, why really? She walked toward me holding something I recognized.

Do you remember the ones in the locust tree?

She paused, looked out the window into the early dark. Turned.

Listen, Agnes. You go find Bruce and you beg him to take you back.

Why would I do that?

He's the only person who's ever been able to love you.

My sister leaned over me on the couch then to spread the quilt, a familiar pink and mustardy yellow patchwork—cotton candy and vomit. One of Ruth's. She tucked me in and kissed my forehead. Bethany had long ago replaced our mother. I would've been a son if I could've but Pop hadn't wanted kids, not of no gender.

I didn't mention Ruth's diary, or her photographs of the two of us. I don't think Bethany's sect believes in images. The walls in her house—plain, unpainted beadboard.

V

Why Agnes bring?

You mean why did I go? You've been pissing me off.

Chapter Two

I'd left Solo enough water and grain but he'd barely touched them. I can't eat either. When I got back from Bethany's, the whole house smelled of death. Still, my appetite shouldn't be affecting his.

I may have to start making more trips to the turkey farm for waste stock. Solo devours that. His feathers were disheveled as if he'd been rolling in the dirt like some mammal. I should've forced him to take that damn bath. Lack of hygiene is not a good sign. It's possible he's molting early—I found some smaller feathers scattered around the barn. Lesser pinions, looks like, terribly small. Some of his primaries these days are as long as my leg, or Bruce's even, though he's not available for comparison.

It's possible Solo's relying on me too heavily, socially. I have to decide what's next for us. Breeding is over. But is he old enough? Tame enough?

You want to fly, Solo?

Bring Solo. Bring.

Yes, Solo, flying can help you disappear.

Chapter Three

A BLOT OF CROWS

⌄

POLAROID: *Agnes—age 6, Bethany—age 4*

In flowered dresses, two girls sit on a bench. The older one, A, has her arm around the younger, B, protectively.

Hard shadows mean late afternoon. The little one squints. Both of the girls wear tight braids. On the cracked sidewalk in front of the bench—the shadow of the photographer, their mother R. The father does not like photographs. It is not a religious qualm, he is not religious. The pictures, she tells them, are for her brothers, though she never sends any. Proof that everyone is just fine. Just fine.

Neither of the girls smiles although they have been posed in a loving tableau.

After the picture, R calls to them to come back to her. They have dressed up to walk the three miles to the country store and they will walk back with their few items. R has picked up some sewing supplies and a five-pound bag of flour. A asks to carry the heavy cloth sack.

It's too heavy for you, R says to the child.

I can do it.

You think you can, but it isn't true. In two minutes you'll just ask me to take it back.

So?

R pauses, steels herself.

You mustn't speak to me that way.

Why not? A is testing something.

The mother is holding B's hand and pulls it up gently to stop the younger, oblivious child. R then turns to her older daughter and lowers her chin.

Listen to me, my brooding one. You cannot give, or take, anything back. Not a single thing that you have said or done—not a thing you ask or are asked to carry.

She scans the path they are heading up. She continues, but to herself.

Time and gravity pull only one direction, downhill.

They start walking. Her mother has given A the bag, and she will carry it for well over an hour. It will be hard for her to keep up, she will stumble, her arms and back will hurt, and her mother will allow her to fall far behind on the long gravel road that leads up to their house. It is a humid day and the girls haven't had anything to eat or drink since breakfast. They know hunger a little, but not the fear of it. Theirs never lasts so long. A will cry but will also stop to clear her face, ridding all evidence of tears. She has almost learned how not to cry but is not there, not yet. When she gets to the porch, she will drop the flour in an act of defiance. It will thud, disturbing any of the small creatures dormant beneath the pine boards—beetles and garter snakes, fieldmice and worms—waking them. She will not bring the bag inside.

R, meanwhile, talks quietly to herself as she does sometimes, walking too quickly for the confused toddler she occasionally tugs forward. B stumbles and recovers. Their mother is clearly upset and A, watching from behind, will try the whole walk long—even as she battles the betrayal of being allowed to carry what she asked to carry—to puzzle out why.

Downhill is a good direction. Sledding in winter is one of the best things, the wind waking her cheeks, the speed, the squeals of B, too scared to try herself but making enough noise for both of them. One might think such shrieking would disperse the watchers in the trees.

But they are never moved.

V

Bruce and I have a few things in common—one is that our parents, derelict in entirely different ways, effectively raised orphans. The other is work. Within two months of moving in, we'd scrubbed and repainted most of the rooms and turned our attention to the barn: cleared out rotting hay, replaced the gutters, patched a hole high on the eastern wall. I was up in the loft when I saw the nest. A mass of twigs lined with what looked to be fur. I counted four olive-speckled turquoise eggs.

Mina wanted to see, but it was impossible to hoist her up the ladder. We waited two full days, her complaining the whole time, until I was sure no mother was coming back. It was a crow's nest—though there were plenty of trees on the property that species should prefer. Bruce joked.

> *Maybe these are fancy crows, crows with inside tastes. Superior crows. Like Leopold and Loeb, evolved beyond the common murder.*

Chapter Three

I might have decided then—while he was busy being clever—to hatch them.

I bought a heat lamp from the farm store, the kind for seed starting and basement cannabis, and brought the nest down into one of the dilapidated horse stalls. Mina came to sit and watch every day for a week. She asked questions. *When will they hatch? How long till they fly? Are they warm enough?* She got worried they wouldn't emerge after I warned her this was a distinct possibility.

When the first egg cracked open, what poked through looked nothing like she expected—this was a blind and gray-tendoned tulip, all throat. She didn't fall in love with the first awkward bird, or the next, or next. She got angry. *They don't even have feathers, they're all wrong, why do they have to look like that?* I knew just what she meant. But these ones were going to be fine. I asked her to help feed them, but that got old quick. Their mouths never quieted, never closed. Instead, she kept on with the questions.

How can they live with no mother?

Better than some with, I said.

One egg did not hatch and its refusal bothered her more deeply than the other, living hungers.

We should bury it.

It happens, Mina. It's part of life.

It isn't. We should bury it like Grandpop.

I handed over the egg but begged off the ceremony Bruce and Mina held in the kitchen garden beside the greenhouse. They'd cleared out both to plant vegetables and herbs, had done this while I was tending the birds.

The other three hatchlings emerged abnormally large. This was some mutation, I was sure of it, if it wasn't cross-breeding with another species—these could be cravens or some other noxious hybrid. By fall they would have scared off the others, crows who'd been roosting on the property since I could remember. So I clipped their wings and kept them in the barn. For a few weeks I slept there with them. They fed constantly. I used an eyedropper first, then my hand. Mina didn't like it when I fed them live things, grubs and grasshoppers, or raw things, meat I chewed up and spat into my palm. She began visiting less, then not at all.

I cobbled together a small lab through the mail. I could still get chemicals and reagents from vendors I knew personally. Growth hormones would do some of the work, and if I could keep the epigenetic switches I flipped on to stay on, well then, the next generation might be truly impressive.

Next I had to speed up their maturity, their breeding cycle. Manipulating circadian rhythms helped with that. More heat lamps: small fake suns.

The old horse stalls had given me my idea. It was of course impossible. Until it wasn't.

V

OCT14

Last night, partly because the reek has seeped beyond the kitchen, I wandered out onto the front porch at dusk. Somebody somewhere was burning something—the faint smoke blissfully sharp and sweet. A few feet from where Ort was found dead, I stood with my glass of brown like an academic . . . one of Bruce's friends spouting Marxist drivel in Italian shoes. There was a moon too, waxing and bright.

A porch is meant to be a place to greet people. But that never really happened here, I was never taught how to welcome anyone in.

Chapter Three

The beauty of this place at this time has always confused me. Autumn. The hidden cricks, the fields, the scrub, the trees, the sky: this is their season. At harvest they become briefly miraculous, able to give rather than take. It's possible I'd imbibed the perfect amount of whiskey, but it was as if everything beyond the porch was dusted in pewter light, cool and warm at once, burnished silver. Even the crows—whose nightly clamor has been intensifying—were for once quiet. They were letting me have this.

It's been raining leaves the past few days. The downed ones walk across the drive or burst into sudden somersault. There's still some green too, pines and the acid-loving rhododendrons beneath. The brightest colors though, the rusts and golds and crimsons, are announcing their exits, broadcasting their abandon. Each year they give up wildly on life while the house remains, proud and drab.

The Krahn property knows no glimmer, it yields nothing—and no matter how much I've wanted to leave it behind, I haven't. I set out but can't *get* out.

I'm alone now, and that feels more honest than anything I have ever done, being alone. If I'm not with people, I can't pull them under. Bethany used to crawl beneath this porch to talk with a little boy who didn't exist, gladder company than me. Called him Toby. Pop whittled dummies out here—crude figures holding spears he said Opa once carved for Oma—their only job to stand eyeless watch on the railing. Sentries I thought, soldiers denying entrance to strangers (everyone not us was a stranger), but ones who would never kill, who didn't have that violence inside them. I knew this because of how many I smashed into splinters.

I threw my glass. It shattered on the gravel drive, and the crows burst into riot. I'm finished. Done wishing for some way in, or out. If edge is my lot—so be it.

V

OCT16

Yesterday I attached to Solo a long leather tether with a choke chain I pieced together from six I bought at the pet store. It took forever, even with Pop's pliers and a vice, the links were so strong. They need to be. I climbed up on the stall to fit it. He balked at first, twisting away, nearly tossing me off the half-wall—but eventually we managed.

Since I've been going there, I've noticed PetMart has everything needed to build a world-class puppy mill. It's amazing to me, the cottage industries that thrive in this unholy corner of the planet.

I was nine, Mina's age, when I was invited to my first and only birthday sleepover. At least, I was one of ten girls from our fourth-grade class this girl had been forced to invite. Ruth fought with Pop—*She should go, see all the fuss, it might cure her of asking for more of it.* The girl's name was Renée.

How exotic that sounded. It was French, Renée bragged, her name. I wanted to be French. Like perfume, like toast, like Marie Curie. Except, no—Marie Curie was Polish. In the biography Ruth had me loan from the library, though it was well above my grade level, it said the last name came from Marie's husband Pierre, as did their research, which killed them both.

I was never going to make that mistake. Marry.

We went out at twilight to catch lightning bugs. I wandered away with my jar because the other girls were having conversations I was unequipped for. Barrettes and batons. I gravitated to a hand-me-down dirt bike. Renée had gotten a brand-new one that day from her dad who sat on his vinyl recliner leering at us the whole party long with a beer in hand Renée's mom kept replacing. The girls went toward the east side of the house—I took off in the other direction.

Chapter Three

Over the hill behind their backyard I found a dirt road and once I got on it I kept going, jar in basket. Maybe I went a mile, maybe two. I stopped a few yards away from the brick shack, close enough anyway to hear. There was just the one window with a stained sheet hanging on the inside. I dropped the bike and my jar fell out. It rolled into the weeds. I left it there and dragged one of the empty crates, strewn everywhere, across the grass. I climbed up on it and pulled the sheet to the side.

It was like a slap, a wall of stench where the windowpane should have been. I squinted hard. Cupped my hand over mouth and nose. Held my breath, leaned forward, peered in.

The moon behind me leaked its malignant light into the bunker. Huge eyes shone out from wire towers in miniature versions of the same: the same moon fractured, multiplied, and caged—two per. Whimpers, howling, ribs rippling with hard breathing, patches of matted fur, the smells of piss, shit, death: all the sensory tells of neglect. Signs Bethany and I did not so much show.

I looked for a few seconds only. I jumped down and sprinted to the bike. I rode as fast as I could back to the house to tell no one what I'd seen. I could imagine no crueler prison, but I had no thought of freeing the animals—they'd been made monster. No good could come back from that.

By the time I returned the girls were in the front yard twirling sparklers. My heart was pounding, I was sweating and panting, but no one had noticed me gone. Some of them were sticking the lit ends into their jars, killing their catches. My jar was lost, sunk beneath the tall grass beside the dark smudge of shack.

One girl had smeared bug juice under her eyes and was doing awkward, inexpert cartwheels across the lawn. She was alone, too, at the party.

No one at PetMart yesterday asked, *Why so many chains?* They don't ever ask, which might be solid policy. It was a struggle to get my handiwork onto Solo, but I managed. I led him out to start training around 9 p.m. Dark, but not completely dark. The moon was low and large, waiting to be divided. A puppy-mill moon.

Not super—just low, near the horizon.

Humans are wired to see things on the horizon as closer than things in the sky. This I assume is because of predation. On the savannah it was the lions. The birds came only after we were done for, only after we were pretty well gone, to pick us clean.

⌄

To equate crow with blackness
is to forget. The white crow
was not the first crow

but existed
and spread its legend across
the sky like piss.

~BN

⌄

Oct29

About two weeks ago I relocated to the barn, only heading back up to the house for supplies. Yesterday, I went up to retrieve a late-afternoon bag of Utz from the pantry, and I couldn't take it anymore. I wrapped a dishtowel around my nose and mouth and I ripped apart the goddamned kitchen.

It took more than an hour, but I located the source. Under the sink, behind the Comet and Clorox and the extra rolls of paper towels—a plastic bag. When I reached to pick it up, it leaked, dripping viscous green-dark slime like out of a zombie's mouth, a thick goo with the consistency of blackstrap molasses and the smell of something long-turned. Long-turned and angry.

I recognized the bag. This was, despite the hellish odor, a few straggling potatoes gone liquid. This was chemistry: anaerobic putrefaction, what happens to organic beings sealed in synthetic prisons. I have no idea why or when I stowed them there behind the cleaning compounds. I'm not absent-minded, but what I do have I once dubbed bottle-fog. In college it stupidly felt like a talent—not-vomiting—instead blacking then passing out before getting the kind of sick that would've saved me a wasted next day. I managed to sop up the black bile from the area around the pipes without losing my stomach. I might've felt better if I had, but I never can seem to let out what's in me.

After I transported the bagful of sewage outside to the trash, I opened every window in the house and went down for our rounds.

Twelve days ago, on his first trip outside the barn, Solo had no idea what I wanted from him. Still doesn't. Maybe I've left it too long and he'll never fledge. I did eventually convince him to arc around the pen in a large loop, less than a week ago. We've walked in circles since. He likes counterclockwise best. Sometimes he opens his wings and I get excited but then he pins them back at his sides and stops to claw the earth. He did this last night. Frustrated, I pushed for an explanation.

What are you doing, Solo?

Solo dig.

I can see that. Why?

Why Solo.

No. Not why Solo—why Solo dig?

A nervous tic, maybe. The grass is gone. I don't suppose we really need the fence I put up but I think it calms him, to have a boundary.

It calmed me to build it. The stench in the house may be bolstering my resolve a bit, but I've always liked being outside. The labs at DDR were never the right place for me: too sterile, too ordered, no windows, the fluorescence flickering too green. I felt big there, poorly contained, awkward and angular, always knocking over something, usually notebooks, but on a few occasions an Erlenmeyer or Florence flask.

I once dropped a vial rack that held dioxins and solvents while I was unknowingly holding Mina, deep and early, inside of me. She knows this story—I've never hidden it. After the accident, the world smelled like a narcissus flower. A small white flower that looks like a bride and reeks of all a bride shouldn't. During the first weeks of my pregnancy in my nose always was a touch of urine and manure and something like paint thinner. A mix of organic and chemical smells that made me think of home: the place where I was born. Solo too. The odor was oddly comforting, nothing like the smell of the molten tubers under the sink. Roots dug up like corpses only to be sealed off and shut away a second time—the dead, forced to suffer death's indignities all over again.

I built the exercise pen down the slope between the barn and the pond. The trees at the edge of the north field block the sightline from the road. We don't need gawkers. I used yellow pine and a split rail design, an easy build. Now, after some practice, with meters of leather looped over my shoulder, I can hold his tether fairly slack in the ring while he circles, except when he starts moving too fast for me. Then I give a tug.

Solo doesn't like that. He isn't supposed to.

When the choke chain burrows under his neck feathers, pushing them askew, it makes him look like an old judge up on his dais—like the fossilized set of robes I appealed my fine to—ruffled I'd even requested a hearing. But I'd parked in the bus zone to carry my daughter into her appointment in the rain and it had been *necessary*. There were supposed to be disability accommodations; everything I'd done was good. Or, not good, but right.

Solo may be my sentence (Bethany would say cross to bear) but my crime was committed long before I came here. And what was it really? I fumbled toxins in the lab, broke them out beyond the hood, and cleaned the mess up maskless, following not one of the posted laminated OSHA protocols.

And why didn't I?

I think I felt invisible. I don't mean something supernatural, god no. My body has the normal volume and mass. It isn't like Mina's body either: egg-fragile, root-twisty. It works fine, it's strong. I tried not to pay attention to it. Around here, people insist sin manifests bodily—in illness, misfortune, deformation—worse if you're without Jesus. The idea's in the water.

I never believed in any of that, but I avoided my body all the same. It was gross matter, largely irrelevant to the way I wanted to function in the world. Unfettered. My physical form was but an essential hindrance . . . in that a chemist needs hands. Ironic really, as apparently my grip is substandard.

This past week Solo's been scratching at the barn wall, not with talon but beak. Though his beak is undeniably sharp, these are not honing actions but a set of purposeful, repetitive etchings. Another tic? I check the marks. I'm not sure for what exactly. His body is different from mine. Moves differently, makes differently.

He doesn't resist the collar anymore. He's learned what's next. The second he gets outside he takes a big breath and puffs up. I'm not sure whether his ribcage expands or there's some shift in his feathers—like hair standing on end—but he grows to nearly twice his size, an illusion which shouldn't affect me as much as it does. Solo, doubled, is the size of a workhorse: a Clydesdale, Belgian draft, Percheron. Every time he does this I wince. I am reminded how much smaller I am than him. Much.

When he engages in this pompous show, I yank the collar as hard as I can, and he deflates. He does this every time. He swole last night, knowing the pain that would follow. I'm certain this is will, that he is willful.

Stop that Solo, I said. And he diminished.

Bring Solo.

I am bringing Solo. Out. So Solo can fly.

Solo fly.

Yes, fly.

He walked for an hour. His head stretches laterally forward at each step, his beak spears the air in front of him. I walk my smaller circle at the center, the line slack between us. He's tested me with speed but not speed for flight, that's not how they take off. Crows need no runway. They lean forward, flattening out their bodies, their heads almost touching ground, legs crouching as they extend their wings—and then they push off. He hasn't tried. I thought if I took him outside and got him moving it would just happen. Despite his size, he is young and curious. But last night all he did was walk, only once stopping to turn to look down at me in the center of the pen.

He said my name. Agnes.

Agnes.

Then, nothing.

After I got him back in his stall, I walked up the path to the dark house. I went in, flicked on the overhead, breathed deep. The smell has faded quite a bit, but I'll be leaving the windows open, same as in the barn—cracked to flung-wide since April. I made my way to the living room and wrapped myself in a thin aquamarine throw Bruce defended his purchase of, saying *more for mood than use* in a house lousy with quilts. I picked up Ruth's book from the table. It felt heavy, but my arms are sore.

Chapter Three

⌄

My Daughters,

Today, Agnes, you sat on my bed and asked me if I am haunted. What a thorny question from my sharp and pokey girl. I told you places are haunted, not people, but I'm not certain that's truth, not entirely.

My dying is an inarguable fact, and I won't be fighting it. Today I want to explain to you how death is at the HEART *of any place so you must not fear it, as it is what lets you see through to any river bottom, its silt and shale.*

		D				
H		E		E		
	E		C			
		A			=	THE CLEAR DEPTH
	L		R			
P		T		T		
		H				

When I write of PLACE, *please don't think I mean this house, or not only this house, though it is a sort of bell jar, a static space, keeping out the flies drawn to the myriad smells of* DEATH *inside. Everything we take into our bodies is already in some state of decay, and this house is the same.*

This house is itself sick, and it is glad that I am sick, otherwise it would not have finally welcomed me into THE CLEAR DEPTH *of its heart, as it finally has. This house considers itself a bulwark—against the birds I'd guess if forced to guess—but there are always barbarians at the gate. I once blamed man's hunt for beauty for all the ugliness of the world, but blame is deception. Winged or wayward, we are all bound up in the same wrongs.*

*In that spirit, I want you to remember that is unwise to hate this house, a thing capable of nurturing you, should it choose to, a thing whose responsibility *is* you. Do not hate such a thing as that. Girls, if you can help it (but perhaps it is obvious that I am speaking most especially to you, Agnes) do not hate, at all. HATRED is the thing that haunts, the THREAD pulling EARTH towards DEA . . .*

The handwriting trails off there—as if she'd fallen asleep writing. This is how she was, how she'd always been. I could almost hear her voice, the sometimes flooded sometimes trickling crick of it running out to its sea of nowhere and coming back, brackish.

Chapter Four

AN ECSTASY OF CROWS

∨

Nov4

Bruce left a voicemail. He wants me to sign the papers. Eight months since he left, nine weeks since he sent them. He says it's time.

It can't have been that long.

Last fall they were here, Bruce cooking most afternoons. When I'd come back from the barn, the house would smell like rosemary or curry and there'd be a plate left in the fridge. He was talking about planting two more beds come spring and filling the greenhouse, something we'd never dreamt of in the city. Harvest had thrilled them, him and Mina. They'd been out all summer long inspecting their peppers and lettuce, their carrots and tomatoes and cucumbers. They learned how to make olive loaf and a cornbread recipe from his nana—sweet and gritty, slathered with local honeybutter. He'd begun complaining about his waistline. He took occasional runs with Mina, who still fit in her old racing stroller, though he'd lost the habit of a schedule.

Time bleeds here. Days overlap. This journal is the only reason I know what month it is. That and the moon.

It must have been last October when we went apple picking. The teenagers working hayride and corn maze were almost entirely zombified, doing spasmodic bits in ripped t-shirts with ultra-white or avocado faces, blackened eyes and teeth. Mina said their moves were not at all convincing, which I found hilarious and Bruce did not. She cracks me up sometimes, that child, how wry and wise she cracks. At the orchard entrance, we were greeted by an older man dressed as Big Boy from the diner chain—checkered overalls, fake belly, rubber pompadour.

Bruce tried. He offered a *Howdy Dude!* The guy deadpanned, *I'm no frick'n ginger*. Then he stared at the two of us with vague, possibly feigned hostility before turning his attentions to Mina. With her, he lit up. She had braids that day, twin black strands of licorice on either shoulder. Her hair is her one trait more me than Bruce, straight not springy, though mine is finer. The old man bent to ask her favorite color, then offered her a piece of stick candy not-that-color. He looked up at us for permission, a bead of sweat rolling from gluey temple to ruddy nose. This was overkill—the kind when strangers don't avoid the disabled and go instead the other way. I could tell Mina didn't want it but Bruce nodded a yes, embarrassed he'd mixed up his clowns. She was polite, too polite, waiting to hand off the candy until we were out in the trees.

We left her chair by the booth and Bruce lifted her up onto his shoulders like he does, wrapping her feet beneath his armpits, her old sling-scarf as securing harness. We'd come apple picking because it was crisp out and blue and Bruce insisted on doing something from my childhood. Something fun.

Did your mom make apple pie?

No. Pop said fruit was sweet enough without the sugar.

So what did you do with your apples?

I told him. We ate them for weeks. Ruth made unsweetened sauce with bits of skin that Bethany and I'd be endlessly fingernailing from between our teeth. Pop would take us over to our one set of neighbors, the Wollners, whose boys he paid to help him hay in the summer months and we weren't to speak to. We looked though.

> *That so?* Bruce raised an eyebrow.
>
> Pete and Eric. Too old to pay us any attention, but our first crushes. I liked Pete, he had a long scar on his forearm, knife throwing accident. Which, now that I think of it, would make Eric the badass.
>
> *There's my girl.* Bruce was nodding his approval. *Loving on us sad boys.*

Bruce has no scars. What he does have is a single tattoo stretching across his upper back, a quote: . . . *the truth is furiously knocking.* Sad boy indeed. Mina made a face up above her dad's. She did not approve of our banter—or didn't want us to know she did.

> Pop fed the mealy apples to the Wollners' hogs while he talked prices. The animals were big by then so no way we'd go near the fence, but he did. After he made his selection, he'd order a side for the winter.
>
> *A side of pork?*
>
> He'd make a deal to go over to help butcher it. Cheaper that way. I asked him why we didn't raise our own.
>
> *What'd he say?*
>
> That he was done with that.
>
> *Pigs?*
>
> Raising things . . . for slaughter. We ate applesauce and ham-and-bean soup all winter. And sauerkraut, though not with caraway. No seeds, he said—*We aren't damn birds.*

Bruce laughed at that.

I won't. I won't be signing the divorce papers. I've decided. He's the goddamned quitter, not me.

I undid the wrapper. The flavor Big Boy shoved at Mina wasn't lime but sour apple. He'd wanted to watch my daughter's face pucker up. Some kids like the sour and some will cry. Either way, the shock of it was his goal—giving a little girl some sensation she wasn't expecting.

The sharpness twanged in my jaw. I should've inserted myself between my daughter and that creep. But I kept sucking—sucking, then shuddering. Mina squinted down at me like I was some kind of idiot.

Why are you eating it if it tastes bad?

Not bad, sour.

But isn't sour how you know something is bad?

And Bruce's huge laugh buffeted our daughter into the sky like a drumbeat.

∨

POLAROID: *Agnes—age 11*

She slips into the cellar to do the wash. Since A's mother has been feeling poorly, the wash has become her job. They have an old machine, and no dryer.

She takes the clothes out of the basket and divides them into their piles: whites, light colors, dark colors of light weight, dark colors of heavier weights, her father's work clothes, woolens to wash by hand with cold water in the utility sink, stained blue. (Later, she will hang them on the line, and this will be the picture R takes from the kitchen: A, standing with legs wide, pulling the clothesline low to pin her sister's and her skirts and small clothes for hoisting up into the wind.)

There is always some action in R's pictures she has been moved to arrest.

A has put the first load in and climbs up on the washer. The washer sighs, the washer hums, her body hums along with the washer. She shudders. Occasionally, her throat lets slip a little sound and she must slap her hand over her mouth.

A is a sinful girl. She knows never to put her hand down there but when she removes it from her mouth that is where her hand goes on its own.

The tang of detergent combined with the fungal musk of the basement: the smell of pleasure as A first came to know it. This was always followed by a trip outside, into the wind-stitched yard by the thorn-barbed locust.

v

Nov7

Solo has been making more marks.

I looked up a story on the internet, about an elephant. Its handlers claimed the animal painted with its trunk, and it did—the same design nearly every time it was given materials. I read about bowerbirds whose nests are elaborate anthems to their mates, decorated with touches of color.

This is not what is happening.

Art is a frivolous human activity, a byproduct of our large brains. Art is about sex, and sex—for all animals—is a futile attempt to avoid death. If animals make something like art it is a sign of their unhealthy relation with humans, a strategy to elicit better treatment, to live longer. That, or it's a courtship excess, evolutionarily selected upon through mating.

My mother made hideous quilts. She knew they were.

Today I moved Solo into his old, smaller stall so I could safely examine his scratchwork. He asked for the crows but I refused. The recordings don't really calm him and their half-legible babble is getting on my nerves, but Solo was insistent.

Tapes.

They're MP3s, but *tapes* isn't as much a beakful.

No Solo, I want to look at what you've done here.

There is an entire room dedicated to Cy Twombly in the basement of the Philadelphia Museum of Art. Bruce took me there during grad school—we did all the things because he wanted to and I wanted to be wanted. I thought I wanted that. Bruce loved Man Ray and Miro, he wanted me to love Horace Pippin and Picabia. But Cy Twombly was his favorite. *A real writer of a painter*, he insisted. *Unapologetic.* I would've said maniac, a lunatic with a crayon. Even his name sounded childish.

He scribbled strange words, often Greek, beside brief stabs or gushes of color.

Solo's work on the barn wall has neither. What it has is the same intensity, the same urgency, the same self-assurance. Solo must believe, like toddlers and Twomblys do, that he has something to say. Mina thought so. I have a picture she gave me when she was four, made at one of those camps in the city Bruce was always signing her up for. It's not good—she lacked the finer motor skills—but there's something that catches you, an idea. It's a picture of our stoop in Kensington, a neighborhood drug-addled and immigrant-heavy. For steps, she drew three rectangles with red flowers to the side in a trapezoidal pot. Everything: two-dimensional. And the three of us, sitting at the top, smiling big smiles more black crayon than white paper behind.

I don't remember ever doing that. Any of it.

I think the pot bothered me most. It had no curve. It was like a shard of some immense ceramic idea of pot and too small a shard: a hint of pot. The picture was a wish. Us, happy. I do get it—I too once believed I had things, forms or futures, things I was supposed to bring into being.

These turned out to be poisons.

Solo's etchings are of two distinct types: straight and crescent gouges. They overlap in places but there's a rhythm to them. They might be mistaken for the script of some lost language or notes on a musical staff. Bruce took me twice to the symphony. We sat listening to a Joplin/Gershwin program on the Mann Center lawn with champagne for our third anniversary and a month later he convinced me to go back for Mahler—which sounded like a storm always a mile away. A year later he brought me down the Jersey Shore to Cape May where we climbed the lighthouse. It was November. I was pregnant. It was my first time at the ocean. We walked hand in hand along the gray shore in the spitting rain. Every bright piece of plastic at my feet was a nod to the world I was entering.

Chemical synthesis. Combining things at their most basic levels. Tones. Colors. Molecules. I will never stop being astonished at the ruin humans visit upon nature because we think we have something to contribute.

I run my hand over Solo's marks. They vary in length and shape and depth. There is a calculus to them I cannot fathom.

They are like Bruce's love.

v

Nov19

He flew. Solo.

Solo flew.

When he lifted off, I unthinkingly dropped his chain. I watched and he disappeared. I stood there, for a long time, waiting. I strained my neck scanning the dark for him before lying down in the pen.

He came back. It's nearly dawn now, a few hours since he landed not a yard from me, startling me awake, broadcasting dirt across my face. I'd pulled a horse blanket over me though the past few days have been unseasonably mild. Still, the earth leeched more warmth from me than was right.

Good, Solo, good—you flew!

I was, am, proud. Prouder than of anything I've ever done. I picked up the dangling tether, sure he'd be hungry. There was a raccoon carcass waiting. I found it near the pond yesterday, mauled by something. Foxes, maybe . . . they can get skittish and run off before they're done. Ruth read to us from Aesop's fables—like Grimms' she said—the stories likely pilfered from foreign servants and nursemaids. I remember an account of a fox who outwitted a crow with flattery. I've never heard a fox speak and I could give a shit who lays claim to a folktale, but it's true Solo can be arrogant. He seemed tired. He let me lead him halfway to the barn before I remembered that, although Solo flew, he flew *away*.

Bad, I said then. I stopped to make sure he heard me. Bad Solo.

Why?

Why bad?

This should've been self-evident, even to him.

Why Solo?

He meant, Why did I need Solo? A stupid question asked by a nearly dumb beast big as a door with eyes flat as bedside cola. Why Solo? Because there's no one else. But I didn't answer him. The brain of a bird can do nothing with such information.

Chapter Four

˅

Voicemail

Mina: Mom, Daddy said I should call—Happy Thanksgiving! Halmoni and Poppy are making a turkey for us . . . they couldn't believe I never had one. Poppy asked me if you were a vegetarian, and I told him you weren't, that you ate everything Daddy cooked, but you only helped with knives sometimes, and not the oven. Halmoni said, Shouldn't a chemist bake? and I said we did once . . . do you remember the cupcakes with the lemon icing? How I did the rind and hurt my hand and Daddy yelled? She said I *should* learn to help and asked me to butter the turkey and it was pimply and gross and I said so. She pulled out a feather, a wet feather right out of the skin, and I don't know why but I got really sad. I cried a little. So we washed my hands and Daddy had me call you. But first I asked him why we never had turkey, and he said this was not a day to celebrate and we talked about Columbus and a man named Zinn and Daddy took out his phone and ordered his book for me, for later. Did you know how many Native Americans died of smallpox? Did you know the Europeans gave it to them *on purpose*? But Daddy says I'm probably only about half-European, your half, and that people don't get smallpox anymore and then he gave me his phone and said I should call you to ask how vaccines work, that he didn't really know until you explained it, and that you are one of the smartest people he's ever met in some ways. Mommy, I love you. I hope you have the best day, even with no turkey. I might not eat any either . . . or maybe I will. Halmoni worked so hard, and Poppy made sweet potato pie.

V

Nov23

I didn't write this down after his flight—I should have. This journal needs to be honest, a full accounting. That much I owe.

I'll write it now.

After Solo made it back to the barn, he began scratching at the wall where he does. But this time the marks were dark. When I touched them, blood. I put my fingers to my tongue to make sure. It's possible he came across some deer mowed down on 222 . . . his kind scavenges. But that's not what I thought. The sign he repeated on the wall looked like a forked twig with the fork downwards. Like a man.

At college I took several nonscience classes. Religion. Literature. History. Latin didn't fit my schedule, so I signed up for a single semester of Japanese. But Solo isn't versed in much language at all, and not written, and nothing but English. This particular split-legged kanji—spoken *hito*—I'd always thought primal. It looked like: bi-ped. A crow might see a human in just such a way.

It's kept me up for days. When I do manage to pass out I have bad dreams: an old-fashioned camera with a shroud over its photographer that won't come off, an apple rotting in a doll's palm, all of Philadelphia burning under liquid fire.

And because I'm not pregnant and cannot be again, there is no place within me for my nightmares to manifest.

Yesterday was Thanksgiving. I left him in the barn while I went to listen for any report that would explain the blood, but it was all parades on the kitchen radio. Once we went as a family to see the Mummers on New Year's, before Bruce discovered it was racist. Mina loved the drums and horns and feathers. It had been a beautiful day—as clear as 9/11—though not as warm.

I got out some pickled beets from the pantry and boiled and mashed a potato. I didn't drink. I went back to the barn later and Solo was restless but I didn't take him out to the pen, not that night. And not tonight either.

Instead I picked up with Ruth again.

∨

Daughters,

You're at school now. Your father says you should be home with me. He and I have been having words. I said not yet.

There are *things school can't teach, most things in fact, but I am of the opinion that you need to be with people. You—not me—as me with people never did work out so well.*

I loved school, right up until I started getting in trouble for asking my questions. I was at an age not so far from your ages now: eleven, twelve maybe. No one seemed able to answer them—I am thinking now no one even tried. I asked: Why had the woods this place was named for been corralled along cricks or ridges? What happened to the treaties? The peaces? The people they were struck against like flint?

Was I truly the only one with questions?

I began looking in libraries and to churches not my own, I read a hundred books and pamphlets, I listened to how people talked and all they said when they didn't. When I first began paying attention, it didn't hurt so much to listen as it does now, the gaps were more patient with me, less like red wounds. I would skip school to climb trees and gaze up inside the sky and stand in streams until my feet wrinkled up all white like pickled fish. Once I took the southern summit trail up Chiquesalunga to look out over the bend in the Susquehanna, but the whole glorious landscape, like the brick front of my childhood house, was merely a façade, *which is French for* FAKE FACE. *And it melted, like faces do, it did. I watched it slough off.*

Did I ever tell you two that I took French in high school because of the kissing? It's true, I have always liked kissing, though your father doesn't think I should speak about things like that, feelings or faces, foreign things. I try not to, for him I try to be quiet, to write the busy thoughts down instead. Did you know that in French hope rhymes with war and moon-ish? That arrows are flesh and this is why they are quivered and sometimes even tipped in copper, the tremblingest of metals? People's skin can shimmer, like faerie lights, like Madame Curie's vials of radium, Agnes, or how Bethany's freckles shift when there's moonlight, the way they dance, threatening escape. We all grow copperlike when we kiss, or are touched, our faces catching in the warm, shivery light.

CUIVRE—*do you see?*

∨

Nov25

Solo's second flight.

I tried to hold on this time. This was a bad idea. My hands are in tatters—I had to bandage them before going back to the pen.

Physics was never my strongest suit—too much abstraction. The breeding of actual (not theoretical) crows is an easier leap for a chemist. Genetics is just a type of cooking: molecular recipes stirred by sex.

Calculating the force of Solo's flight, on the other hand, is a physics problem. Apparently one beyond my meager capabilities.

He came back this time at dawn. He was carrying a reflector—the kind you attach to bikes for riding dark country roads at night. Roads like these roads, with maybe some rhubarb or strawberries in the basket, stolen from a neighbor's garden. The Marquette brothers', for an example, because they were lecherous halfwits who stuck their tongues through their fingers to make Bethany cry and so more than deserved the soap-vinegar-salt treatment I applied to their patches after harvesting my sister's due.

Solo landed and walked over to me and I stood up achy, shaking frost from my blanket with throbbing hands. He dropped the shiny thing at my feet. When I went to pick it up I saw I'd bled through my gauze. The contraption was faceted like an insect's eye and twisted: its leg—black plastic and cheap metal—wrenched and snapped. The large sharp pliers of Solo's beak curved over my head.

Where did you get this Solo?

Solo bring.

Yes, Solo, you went away. But where did you get this?

I shook it at him. Not unkindly. My hand felt like a mitten filled with blood. I knew the thing was a gift. An apology for leaving me.

Crows can't smile. But when he cracks his mouth and raises his head up for a moment, when he makes the whirring, growling, cooing, and clicking combination he should use for courting his own kind, when he paws the ground softly (not quite digging), then lowers his head like a horse bowed for affection, I sense Solo is happy. He may think I belong to him—or him me—in whatever his approximation of thought might be.

He brought me a peace offering. I removed the tether and choke chain gingerly. They are of no use. We walked slowly to the barn, him behind me in engorged shadow. I placed the present on my desk in the corner, next to my engagement ring. They look alike. The bird has been observing my habits, my preferences.

Solo paused over me before moving to the wall to take his notes. My hands were so swollen I didn't try to put on my ring. But despite the pain, I wrote. For a short time we scratched together in the companionable quiet. After that, I went to the house for some sleep though sleep in this house is uneasy. Crows prefer to sleep in each other's company. Hundreds of them haunting a single tree. I've spent most nights this month on a pallet in the barn not far from Solo, but it's getting cold, even with the space heater. I am well aware that every time I leave the barn I prevent him from rest. This morning neither of us will have the peace we crave.

He could kill me at will. The physics are clear. It's important for him to remember that he relies on me for comfort.

I will not give up on his training. Soon, it has to be soon, I will introduce the concept of a passenger to him. I've designed a weighted harness to strap over his back.

Steed/stead/stand/stance.

I am Daedalus. This should be obvious.

V

GIRLS,

PLACE, as you know it, is inescapable, and HISTORY its collective noun. Think congregation of sparrows, quiver of flèches, skulk of foxes, field of daughters. Such a HISTORY has a thousand grasping limbs. You know the centipedes in the basement, so I know you know what I am talking about, but you must not trap and kill these like you do, Agnes, ripping legs off one by one until they grow finally still. They keep the house clear of far worse.

Your father's people knew about this PLACE, knew and stayed. I never met her living, but even still, I've gotten to know your Oma—I've saved her notebooks for you. Your father calls her a charlatan, but his mother was no fraud, not in the slightest. No. She was a spider, trapping as many flies in this house as she could stomach. Of course, one spider can eat only so much before it explodes into a thousand baby spiders, a crèche of infant spiders, all equally hungry, all architects of appetite.

Sadly, Oma was able to birth just one child—Ort. How disappointing that must have been for her.

PLACE cannot be transcended. We are grown from its soils, we drink its waters, we inhale its perfumes and its poisons, and they are legion. A PLACE may prove by turns greedy, tragic, terrified, bleak, and shameful. Despite that, despite all of it . . .

You yourselves must be shameless.

Sometimes when I close this book of hers, I feel something other than rage. But feeling anything for her at all—it's addictive.

Chapter Four

⌄

Nov30

This evening I found my desk chair knocked over in the barn. I shut the windows and made a note to look for loose boards and check the insulation. Winter's nearly here.

I wish it would snow and not just bluster about it. The branches are bare, some blown down, ripe for whittling. Lately the crows' racket has been so loud . . . it's as if they're performing for me, though I stopped recording them weeks ago.

Pop sat out whittling on the porch in all seasons, swelter or frigid bleak, it didn't matter. Inside, Ruth would alternately stare half-way across a room for hours or make herself noisily, manically busy. Nattering: that's what Pop called it. I used to think he was saying *mattering*. Cleaning or cooking or sewing or reading aloud to no one—but this was no show—it was desperation, her way to avoid being. Until she couldn't avoid it. And then she was, briefly, a burning wick of being.

And then she was not.

Chapter Five

AN UTTERANCE OF CROWS

⌄

Dec8

Pop never owned a TV, and we made the decision not to bring one. I have my laptop and his old radio I listen to mornings. I like adjusting the wonky knobs while I make coffee. Pop didn't drink coffee. He maintained a long list of nos—nevers and stoppens and donts.

I make coffee where I shouldn't: Pop's kitchen, out in the barn, in the DDR lab though it was verboten. I told my boss, Dr. Fahmy, he needed ignore this minor lapse because it made everyone around me safer. Spirit of the law. My directness made him nervous, and my jeans, which I wore tight because I'd grown up hiding everything.

Manipulation can feel good. Sometimes it even feels righteous.

Maybe that's why politicians do it—addicts to power and, yes, to feeling virtuous. *Doing* virtue is not nearly as rewarding, neurochemically, plus it's almost impossible to extrapolate the result of a given action out in the world.

Lately, I've been thinking that doesn't necessarily release you from the effort.

I was raised in the blood-red heart of a purple state. Bruce grew up a drop of darker roast in a skim-latte suburb. His words. I think poetry was his idea of rebellion from lawyer parents in Baltimore: LOC—Liberals of Color. The Nobles helped with Mina's lawsuit. Maybe they qualify as good people, maybe. Bruce couldn't live their way, wasn't about to try to fix a system obviously broken. That's a funny stance to take I think, what with Mina, me.

Still, he watches the news, he cares. I can't listen to those stations since he's gone. Just our local. Today another sexual assault case at the courthouse. A young mother, beaten too. Jesus, what is it with this place? Here are the churches, here are the steeples, open them up, see all the rapists.

Vietnam was Pop's fuck-you to hypocrisy. He wasn't drafted, he volunteered. He didn't talk much, but when I asked him about the killings, he told me they were more honest than the whuppings of his childhood. *The military told me who to kill and I did it—it was wrong, never pretended otherwise.* He listed his kills. With gun. With grenade. With bayonet. By hand. Pop's hands were huge, his answers few. I was a curious child, used to his silence, resigned to it in fact, and somehow this one question he chose to respond to.

You don't have to beat a daughter to hurt her. Just wrap her dreams in the plastics of your past—they'll rot. Become impenetrable, apocalyptic muck.

Ruth told us her own father had exhibited none of Pop's restraint. Told us Pop was kinder than we knew. I was old enough when she said that to call bullshit. *Agnes, kindness can be invisible work, but it's still hard.* When she said this, I was young enough to think invisible meant ghosts, and hers not his—because she was the one talking to them.

All of our grandparents died before Bethany and I could know them. Pop was an only, but Ruth had four brothers who lived close-by with their kids. She'd chat over the sink with the dead (I assume), but we rarely saw the living Cullens. She made sure none of them knew she was sick until she was gone. Maybe that's what she meant by kindness.

They're a pack of animals. Pop said this when pressed early on for a reason we didn't visit. Why no one came to visit us. We didn't see others, we didn't take from others, we didn't need others. It wasn't hypocritical but it was lonely. The single time Pop met Bruce, at Bethany's wedding, Pop asked him if he spoke gook or ghetto. Later Bruce referred to him as a *reluctant celebrant.* He was, in fact, a reluctant human.

The rape case on the radio isn't incest though the guy had been living with the family for over a year. Down on his luck but did odd jobs, paid some rent, babysat for free—so I guess there's that. The blame is there if you listen. I think it's a tossup whether you run into, not even good, but decent people. Invite them into your home. Marry them. Are born to them.

After the courthouse material is exhausted and a local fire covered, the announcer segues to human interest:

> *In other news, there was a sighting of* AN ENORMOUS BAT *in Marietta last night. You heard that right. The* SWOOPING BLACK BEAST *attacked two teens who'd stopped at a local playground on their way home from musical practice, *Newsies*, in fact. I know, I know. At least it's not *Seussical*, right? Listen, I know some of you are deeply happy with our newly thriving dispensaries, what with your glaucoma and your back pain. But folks . . . maybe invest in a padlock for your stash? Especially if you have kids of the theatrical persuasion. Police reported the teenagers as* BADLY SHAKEN. *Winners, in all seriousness, *please* secure your bud: this generation clearly can't handle the doobage.*

Winners is what the guys at WINR—and they're all guys—call themselves and the listeners they encourage to call in. Pop listened every day but never dialed. Back when I was in high school he referred to the callers-in as *whiners*. It should have been a joke, warring puns on the station's letters. But Pop didn't joke. The implication was that people were always bitching about something or other. He didn't use that word, but it's what he meant.

Pop didn't believe in complaining. He once told me: *There's no such thing as good and bad—just life, and those too weak to live it.*

V

POLAROID: *Agnes—age 13*

R is dead. Relatives A has never met come to the viewing. They cry. They cry more than B and A have cried in their lives. *We're Irish*, R said. And she didn't mean her daughters; she meant her family. They were Catholic but R wasn't, so no mass. Her husband wasn't having it.

The family stands in the stark air outside of the funeral home, crying and laughing and talking about R when she was young, a girl A doesn't recognize: *Root* they call her, *our Root*. They say she was vivid as flame, then contrary and moody, then strange and gone. Then—surprising all of them—she came back, though not to them. Two of A's older boy-cousins are smoking cigarettes out on the curb in the middle of town in trousers and ties. That she finds herself attracted to one of them confirms everything A has learned to think about herself.

There is no burial and no reception. Their father invites no one back to the house. He doesn't want people coming over with raisin pie. What happened to R that she married this man?

We don't need that.

He is right, B and A don't need raisin pie. B probably wants to cry although she isn't crying, which surprises A. A would like to smoke cigarettes with Tommy and Dolan, but it's too risky. That day, in the parking lot behind the funeral parlor, she drinks from a flask offered by her cousin Jack and tells anyone listening that she's getting out of this place. Only unlike her mother, she's never coming back.

There's another picture somewhere of her and the boys. B took it with R's camera. A doesn't remember, but she did take a drag. The cigarette is there, in her hand.

V

There was a swatch of cotton in the barn. A small swatch, close Swiss dots on a Kelly green field. I have it now. It's rough cotton, stiffer than you'd think.

Not fifteen minutes ago I asked Solo—

> What is this?
>
> *Bring.*
>
> I know you brought it Solo. Where is it from?

More scratches on the wall, frenetic. Solo didn't touch the grain I poured into the trough this morning. The reflector's on my desk beside my ring—one large eye, one small—watching Solo better than I've been able to. I pressed him.

> Solo, what have you been doing?

In answer, Solo walked slowly to the barn door. His shadowy body swayed from side to side but his head moved forward in short jabs. He paused. Then he used his beak to lift the latch and pushed the top of his head against the wood. It swung wide. He looked back. His eyes, at first empty, went milky blue, nictitating membranes pulling across the pupils like camera shutters. He took a few steps forward and stood outside the doorway. He rotated his head 180 degrees, pointing his beak over his back.

Chapter Five

Solo. Don't.

Bruce once dragged me to an outdoor film festival in Princeton—Valentino, Fairbanks, Flynn. Solo tilted his swiveled head like a silent actor regretfully removing his hat, taking his leave. He then turned into the twilight, lowered his chest to the earth, lifted.

And was gone.

v

DEC9

It's late. I'm in the house. Solo hasn't come back and the barn is accusatory.

Sometime last week was Pop's death-iversary. I don't know the actual date. The mailman found him on the porch. Bethany said it was good at least that it was cold.

At 150 years, the house is not the oldest around here. It's old enough. And the Krahn family has lived in Pennsylvania even longer than that, having moved to Letort from Bird-in-Hand after some unspoken-of congregational dispute. The house has been in the family for six generations but, beyond me and Bethany, there are no more Krahns. Pop's birth nearly killed his mother. After that, Oma did her best to occupy herself with other peoples' pain. She never forgave her son for depriving her of better, less faithless children.

Except for its gray porch, the Krahn house is the color of lard, layers of glutinous ivory inside and out.

Ruth cooked with lard until she could no longer stand to cook. She was that thin, despite the food Bethany and I kept bringing her to eat when *to eat* was only a prolonging. People were giving up lard back then. For the heart. Too many farmers keeling over in fields, mothers stroked out peeling potatoes. Ruth cooked with lard until she couldn't, and still her heart refused to stop beating. We had three years of its refusal.

Our favorite meal though, was fried egg noodles. These she made with butter, not lard. Birthday noodles—special noodles for special noodle occasions. Other mothers, Ruth told us, did not caramelize their onions. We did not know other mothers. In the decades after her death, the house's lace curtains grew yellow. The light they filtered in, rancid.

One of the first things Bruce and I did was replace them with wooden blinds. These have lately accumulated a thick layer of dust. I'm no homemaker. It's not a thing I wanted—Bruce knew that.

Ruth's illness began with pain. She couldn't hide it though I've never met a woman more magnetic alive than she was dying: dark-haired, light-eyed, freckled. There must have been a logic to her marrying my father, twenty-six years her senior, but I never figured it. Some box he checked off in her life, some self-punishment she achieved in choosing him. She'd gotten out. Briefly. Then returned. Two years she spent in a girl's college on the Main Line studying art—drawing, painting, textile design.

It was art that was the dead end she said. Art, not lard, Ruth insisted, killed her.

I was always dyeing to die.

When she laughed it was like sugar, a thing we weren't given, hardly ever.

Sugar is a sickness, your father says, and we listen to your father.

Neither sweet nor fat killed my mother. Neither joy nor plenty. She claimed it was her experiments (Ruth called it play) with imported indigo. Pop said cancer—Oma, too, had died of cancer.

One day I fell down from pain. But by then everything was blue.

Chapter Five

The day Ruth finally let go, three years after that first fall, was not blue. There had never been a grayer day, a whiter one. It was February, the morning after a deep snow and the day before the next, the cloud cover staying put. The ambulance couldn't get to us until late afternoon. Pop had us bring chairs in to sit with her, all of us together in that small room, Bethany sobbing.

The crows were there too, roosting in the locust. They stayed on our property all winter. All the winters. Hundreds of crows—hundreds of angry black marks waiting, for what? Ruth kept a book, *The Ornithology Society of Southeast Pennsylvania*, under her bed with the wool-mice. Seems this large band of crows had been coming to our home for a century of winters and only three with her sick. Those three might as well have been a hundred—how dark they were, how long. How heavily annotated: notes scrawled in the margins, her bright blue ink.

Once she died, I took it upon myself to feed the crows. I stole seed from the barn. Pop thought it was rats, and we had them. He would've hurt me for stealing, I'm sure of it. He didn't notice. He hated those birds but he never cut down their tree, not even as it died, each spring after Ruth producing fewer and fewer leaves.

After she was gone, the man mostly left us to our own devices—he just made sure they were separate. Ruth died, and at first Bethany and I held each other in the same bed we'd always shared, under the same ocean-colored quilt with a sickly melon rickrack until he stopped it. Yanked the covers off us in the middle of the night.

> *You're too—get out. I told her.* He was muttering, shaking.
> *Too close.*

He stopped it, as he stopped most things, with shame. We were dirty I learned from Pop because we had skin. We were still intertwined then, how sisters are without realizing, oblivious to limbs and lives braided together. He pruned us. Physically pulled us apart—separate beds, separate rooms, separate grief.

That must've been when we started to grow so different.

I don't know if Pop loved his wife or she him. I remember before she couldn't anymore how she made us laugh and how she laughed with us. Unabashedly. And how that made her dying a betrayal. She had time. She had three years to plot our escape from him, to find us a way out. She didn't.

Mina will be able to get away. Working legs or no, she will have an escape hatch. I've provided it. She will have Solo and Solo will be better for her than any mother.

A mother is a luxury. You had yours plenty long.

Pop spoke little. We were to listen to him. Our mother was like butter, like sugar. We didn't deserve her.

Who deserves the sky?

v

Moons

There are 13 full moons each year, not 12, which means there is a hidden month. Moons are named locally, in accordance with surrounding nature, circumstance, and spirit. I have started with the one that arrives after the solstice, a difficult time to hold onto one's words, to corral them into their correct boxes and sentences, pots and cabinets. It is crucial to be cognizant, also, that once a woman becomes a woman, every moon that isn't filling her up with child is turning her insides out. ~RK

Long Moon—bleared oval, dripping through the southern window
Weeping Moon—for false thaws and clarity

Chapter Five

Green Moon—any glimpse of spring taken back with interest

Stitching Moon—girls who run outside until they cannot and fall into bed like mown flowers

Moon of Woe—for Wednesday's child, named Agnes after some animal

Tomato Moon—ripening, redness, salt on a slice, a moon for intercourse, berries, manure

Hidden Wasp Moon—for the bluehouse, house of figs, for Bethany, sick sweetness, honeysuckling, scents that sour

Maggot Moon—how life departs without ceremony, how flies, how fungi bloom from flesh

Dyeing Moon—returning in stain and trace

Painted Moon—girls growing slack with too much knowing, faces needing fixed

Moon of Ordering—all things put to bed, sown, sewn shut, behind the walls

Frigid Moon—no quilt suffices

Talking Moon—beshrouded, the crows talk all winter and eat, they eat and eat and still they demand more

∨

Bruce gave Mina a book last Christmas Eve he didn't show to me beforehand. I knew why. When I was with them in the house, I heard myself sounding more and more like Ort. Silent—or, if not, then disapproving. He once told Ruth that she'd dyed Bethany's and my skirts *a harlot blue.*

But blue is not red.

So I saw the book when my daughter did. An elaborate woodcut of a black bird sprawled across the cover, muscular feathers curled around the binding. The tale was of Rainbow Crow. Bruce was proud of his find. The story was from the Lenni Lenape he told Mina, the Native Americans whose land Philadelphia sits on, the city where she was born, in a rowhome just a few blocks from the Delaware. I stopped him there with a look. He didn't have to listen to my glare, but he did.

Mina wanted to read it to us immediately. We learned, through her impromptu multivocal performance, how the brave bird consulted with other animals, owl and coyote and turtle, then took it upon himself to travel to the gods when a cold winter wouldn't end. How he lost his voice and his vibrant plumage bringing fire to the world. How he was never the same after that, how only fiercest sunlight revealed the colors of his past, glinting from iridescent feathers.

Mina loved the book. It made sense to her.

That's why they croak. That's why they're so mean.

A bird isn't mean, Mina. It's territorial.

They are mean. They steal things. One from the tree took the suncatchers Dad and I put in the garden.

Suncatchers?

We showed them to you. The copper dragonflies with the glass eyes.

Why didn't I hear about this? I looked at Bruce. He shrugged.

Mina was a force, Bruce's unspoken anger spiraling through her like a funnel. She'd grown older than I'd realized—potentially this was a side-effect of her condition.

You don't listen. She shook her head like a professor. *You don't know anything about us anymore.*

What are you talking about?

Not since the ones in the barn stole you.

If gods existed, I might make a pilgrimage to ask them why they thought an eight-year-old girl the best conduit for their cruelty. Why my husband's words out of his own mouth weren't enough to hurt me, enough.

So that was Christmas. Solo didn't hatch until late March. His mother was proving a handful all winter with her rages, but she was large and healthy and full of purpose—she wanted to fly. Unlike the rest of the crows, she never acclimated to her clipped wings. She beat them against her sides often, and often until she collapsed. One February morning, soon after Bruce and Mina left, she mated with then killed her first son while his sister cowered in the next stall, and I knew we were reaching the end of the genetic line. There was only one viable egg in the resulting clutch. During Solo's first few weeks of life, I grew worried she would attack him next.

Solo was Mina's last chance at flight. I had to put his mother down.

From winter into spring, my childhood started coming back to me in rags and shards. A flash here, a drizzle there. But sometimes I'd get pelted by a hailstone of a size that could shatter a greenhouse panel or snap the bone of a wrist.

v

Decio

On my phone and radio this morning: *Six-year-old Scylla Durfee was last seen playing in front of her house twenty-two hours ago.*

Third Amber Alert this month.

People lose people around here. It's a measurable thing. Girls maybe go missing because of the trucks that pass through. Maybe because of fabled powwowers in the woods. Or because who wants to stay? The littlest missings are usually custody cases, but Scylla's parents are on the news together—transplants from DC, overeducated back-to-the-land types, the father a fracking lobbyist. The announcer rolls the tape: the parents are taking turns reading their script.

> Please, if you know anything at all about where this child is, contact the authorities . . . *Scylla is our first, our pride and joy* . . . She is a smart girl, a clever girl, her sisters are already missing her—she should be home . . . *Scylla likes unicorns and ice cream, her favorite flavor is strawberry, her favorite color pink, she wears a teardrop necklace* . . . We need her back, it is essential we get her back, she may be hurt, we do not want her hurt . . . *She doesn't have her favorite toy, she can't sleep without her stuffed elephant, Chunk* . . . She is a small girl, six, a small six but a big help with her sisters, they will worry if she is away too long . . . *Please, return our angel to us, we need her at home, she belongs to us, with us, at home.*

The announcer comes back on: *If you have any information on this child's disappearance, please call* 888-*WINR*. He's using the more serious voice he vacates when delivering traffic reports or sports commentary. When he reports on those, he's all buddy-buddy. I've never heard a plea like theirs before, not on this station. They must've hired someone.

Does Mina still have a favorite toy? Mint chocolate chip I know. And difficult as it may be for her, my daughter has always liked to draw.

v

DEC11

I cut my foot on a piece of plate this morning. I left a bleary trail on the kitchen tile while ragging up the blood.

Solo has been gone too long. I'm worried. Which is not the same thing as scared.

Chapter Five

Pop once put his hand through a window after hurling a bowl into the kitchen fireplace.

At dinner Ruth had asked him, *What's wrong with your face?* When he wouldn't answer—there was nothing wrong with it—she insisted it had gone soft and was sliding down his forehead. She giggled like a girl. *I can sew it back on . . . backstitch, I think.* She headed to the cupboard for needle and thread. She told him to put his cheek down on the table, and when he didn't, she said, *Girls, help your father.*

His look across the table was paralyzing.

She came back with her sewing kit and pushed gently on the back of his head. This was his limit. He slammed his hands into the table and stood. He towered over her by near a foot, but she smiled up at him, taunting. *Don't be a child, I won't hurt you.* First he threw his dinner, then his fist. But not at her. He punched through the window. He wrapped his bloody hand in a linen napkin, egg blue.

Ruth was so often the cause. But she also knew how to manage his outbursts—soft words, streams of them in her soothing lilt. The content didn't seem to matter. My sister's instinct at these moments was to flee. I was ready to strike but never got to. In this house, I dealt only in aftermath. Ruth swerved, Bethany hid, I swept up what was broken.

I wasn't thorough though, not like Bethany, and Pfaltzgraff wounds run deep. If Ruth had wanted treatment—for whatever ailed her—the surgeon's scalpel might have been made of ceramic. Ceramic plates and blades, minded, last and last.

Solo took off Thursday at dusk toward the east. It's early Sunday morning now and frigid. The cold doesn't matter: the buggies will be out on the other side of Lancaster, black-wheeled beetles moving across snow-dusted back roads to church or for visiting. Will the drivers find him on the side of the road and stop as they would for a fallen horse? But he's not dead. Solo's size would make that news and I've been listening. No, he's in hiding, punishing me for doubting him. Yesterday, I walked out across our neglected acres to see if he'd come back injured.

Because of my foot, this morning I stayed put and turned on the radio—to listen for sightings of the bird. Alive or no. A faint tinge of rot still hangs in the corners of the kitchen . . . or some hard-to-scrub memory of it.

There's been a work stoppage at Salyers. This isn't news except that the trucks keep coming in and aren't being unloaded during a cold snap that's only intensifying. They said the chickens might die, die out in the trucks instead of inside the factory. Die in the wrong place. A hundred thousand misplaced deaths. Feathers like dirty snow.

The woman who called in had a strong accent—maybe Guatemalan? Seems the backup killer walked out too early. Usually there'd be a backup backup killer on the premises, a worker whose job is to step in and stab chickens that had avoided the neck slitter, but not yesterday. She told WINR that the workers have been gearing up for a strike, but both the backup killer and the backup backup had walked out early, and the rest weren't ready. She was livid.

> *A strike?* the announcer was incredulous. *Don't you all make good enough money already?*

The woman snorted. She took a moment of dead air before responding.

> *You work. You work one week, one week on the floor, you tell me after about money.*

They cut to commercial. Too many listeners around here work at the factories—or have family that does—to have him and her go at it. It's not a political station, except for the syndicated assholes. Weekdays I can't listen past noon.

Chapter Five

There are a handful of poultry processing plants in the area, small to large. Pop said they used to hire Amish and Mennonite to undercut labor prices in other parts of the country. He said this with pride. His people had a strong work ethic, wouldn't unionize, weren't squeamish.

Fact is, since the eighties there's been a steady influx of families from Central America working just as hard for longer hours. Not something Pop would admit.

No one I knew growing up set out to work in the factories. They were where you ended up if you got stuck, a red-rivered purgatory. Wastewater channels run through all the plants, ferrying away the foul matter sluiced from hens along with other things. These rivers, like illness, can erode a person.

I lost two months at Salyers the summer after my first year at college. I lied at my interview, said I was quitting school to come back and help out at home. I told them, I'm looking for a stable job where I can work hard and be fairly promoted. I practiced the lie in the bathroom mirror. I planned on taking the overtime and moving off campus in the fall.

Bethany, at least, was happy to have me back.

Salyers is a family concern and Beau Salyers pegged me as managerial, maybe because he could tell I was lying. Plus I was white—to him, a qualification. It's an old-fashioned con, starting me at the bottom but promising speedy advancement.

Listen, don't disclose your hourly.

He'd said this with his hand on my wrist.

It's a little inflated . . . due to your time at college.

He moved his hand up past my elbow—to gauge my interest. I had none. He was soft, he was slime, he lied: my pay was higher than many of my coworkers', it was also lower than that of the white-boy-with-a-GED. We disclosed.

Our crew of six hung the newly arrived and already shackled live broilers upside down on the conveyor belt. They squawked and growled. Clucks, I learned, are the happier sounds. The birds flapped their wings at us too, pointlessly.

Our backup killer worked in one of the next rooms, after Stunning and Slitting but before Scalding. He sat alone during breaks, like me. I couldn't join in the lightning breakroom banter so listened instead to a thrift-shop Walkman while I ate the lunches Bethany packed. That summer I consumed Lebanon bologna on Stroehmann's with Hellman's and French's, as well as Hole and Nirvana and Cake. GED-boy called me antisocial. He was too dull or bigoted to learn the few Spanish phrases I picked up to get along. *Perdoname* and *cuidado* and *que mierda* and some others I've forgotten. The music helped fill blank time and mute the hen noise.

There was no escaping that smell though, for any of us. Or maybe the birds managed to—depending on how you look at it. Their dying.

After two months Beau moved me further inside: the promised promotion. I was to supervise Evisceration. I quit two days after my reassignment and it wasn't the birds. It wasn't even him grazing my ass when he walked past my station, fuckwit that he was. It was my coworkers' eyes—all that was visible of them above their masks. Bodies, even chicken bodies, are terrifyingly unique. Their swift disembowelment requires a mind-numbing concentration. I watched human eyes, filled with death and intent, using the latter to deliver the former. I watched the line of their gaze, marking the paths of knives brought down, and then the yank, insides suddenly out. Spilt. This new room was a highly skilled room. The work—focused and efficient.

I went back to college early. Rented a back room from a retiree named Miss Deb for almost nothing and errands.

Why would Solo want to hurt me like this?

When we were first together, Bruce told me I would never stop being tragic until I faced my trauma.

And which trauma is that?

That made him laugh.

*You are, no lie, the most stoic person I've ever met *not* from my mother's family.*

That's an accomplishment, yes?

We clinked our drinks and later that night made love. He never overdid. I miss that, not his perfect moderation—because what kind of a thing is that for a poet to lay claim to?—but sex. I miss it like crazy. That was before Mina. Before I ruined us by giving birth to her. I did it poorly. I did it in the wrong place. My daughter's birth was a misplaced birth.

I have never been so scared. Someone should have warned me.

Cuidado.

Watch out, watch out for the river of blood.

∨

The day before they left, I walked into the house around 11 p.m., long past Mina's bedtime. Bruce was in the kitchen, where he'd wait when he decided to wait up for me.

What the fuck, Ness. He wasn't referring to the hour.

It's nothing.

The hell it is. Your face—

She wouldn't calm. I thought she was going to hurt herself.

Solo's mother had been erratic all day, beating wings, squawking at her frail daughter in the next stall, clawing at the wooden partitions. I'd finally gone in at dusk, hoping she'd tired herself out—physical contact could sometimes soothe her. I opened the half-door and reached out toward her. She reared up, lifting and twisting her head away from me, haughtily, as if I hadn't earned the right to touch her. Then, without warning, she pivoted to the side, clocking me diagonally across the temple with her wing. I blacked out. There's more power in those things than you might imagine. More than I did.

When I came to, it was fully dark and she was above me, nervously stepping from foot to foot, talons scraping the earth beside my head. I eased my way out of her pen without standing. It seemed wise just then to exhibit deference, though it wasn't my usual practice.

Your eye's swollen shut.

I held some snow on it. It'll be fine.

That thing needs to be put down. They all do. You'd kill a dog that did that . . . What if one gets out?

They can't fly.

Of course he'd want to get rid of them. In his mind, it was past time—the crows, a game I should be done playing, a hobby overreach. To him, the birds were no more than a pottery habit or a home brewery. He certainly didn't see the crows as Mina's wings, her chance to escape us, this horror show. That purpose I'd kept private. It was my gift to her, one I knew would alarm him.

His thinking was simple. Because I'd chosen a questionable career at an *evil* corporation with a history of harm, I should be using this time to rethink my life choices, even if science is the one thing I've ever known how to do. And because I inadvertently poisoned our daughter, he would take over her care utterly, be her primary.

Obviously. And if—miraculously—I'd found a way to stay sane in this godforsaken place while he played nursemaid, governess, and martyr? Well, no doubt that should be taken from me too. For my own wellbeing, the family's.

This isn't what you stayed up to say to me.

He looked down at the table, at his hands clasped in front of him in the shape of grace, a thing we didn't do.

My parents found a summer camp for Mina. They want to pay.

She can't—

She can. Two weeks in the Shenandoah Valley. There's swimming, hiking, crafts—all of it. Each camper is assigned a person.

That must be astronomically expensive.

They want to do it, and she'll love it. You know she will. I'm thinking . . . maybe it's time we visit, spend some time. Mina doesn't really know her grandparents.

I can't leave the birds.

I know . . . that you think that.

He couldn't even say it—that he wanted to take our daughter and leave, cut his losses. The coward.

I told you you'd hate this place.

You did. You *didn't* tell me the minute we got here you'd hole up in some bunker.

It's a barn.

You disappear.

This was unfair. He dropped down his own rabbit holes plenty—his books or his laptop, a clever-enough phone.

Like you, writing?

Not the same, Ness. You go off and there's no calling you home. You disconnect—from us, the world. You're just . . . gone.

> You're so right. What've I been thinking? It's so clear, now that you've said. I should be in the house, maybe knitting socks for Mina's shoeless feet, or out on the frontlines like you are—fighting mass incarceration with haiku.

He closed his eyes, took a deep breath in through his nose and out through his mouth. His shoulders dropped. Fuck his fucking yoga. He went upstairs. I opened the freezer and got a bag of peas for my eye. I slept on the couch, and my husband and my daughter left the next day. For Mina's sake, we treated the trip as temporary. I helped Bruce pack like it wasn't.

v

Crow: another word
for shadow, a shape
through which

light is withheld.

~BN

v

DEC13

Maybe this is a Christmas story.

Solo left me a gift outside the barn, a large red-tailed hawk, light brown with a speckled chest and cream underbelly, neck snapped but otherwise intact—an exceptional specimen. Its sharp, comma-shaped beak would've given it an aristocratic aspect perched high in some pine. A crow's look, even a normal crow's, has more cunning.

Chapter Five

Solo hadn't eaten any of his kill. A remarkable show of willpower. What *is* he eating out there in the world? Where is he sleeping? How is he managing on his own?

Corvids, like wolves, are social animals. Isolated they can go mad, if it's madness to act outside the norm. Bruce—if he were here—would remind me that the word *norm* is meaningless, a tautology proved and disproved only by the social success (or failure) that defines it. When Mina didn't fit any norm, my husband stopped believing in them. But that's not how things work. Statistics aren't Santa Claus.

Bruce would say we're all lone wolves now, howling into the dark of our screens. Ghosts-in-our-own-machines without knowing we are, driving ourselves and each other round the digital bend in search of an outrage that suits us. All that poison piped into our homes on the daily, jacked in. *We've been co-opted*, he'd say. *Popping op-eds like opioids*. Always with the language.

Bruce can go on a rant. I blame his fellow poets—clever, horrible people—as evidenced by him preferring my company to theirs for a decade or more. But rail as he might, my husband has never turned off his own approval apparatus, never unhooked himself. He says he's networking, promoting his words in the only way available to him, that he can't reverse the world's spin. His parents may believe they can change things he says but that's only because they're boomers. Delusional neoliberal bougie do-gooders.

Bruce has his black moods. There were reasons we were together.

I suppose it's possible that online is how Mina will find her people. The new school can't be easy for her, not that part. Friends. I haven't talked to her since Thanksgiving.

The thing I need her to understand is that what I've done, all I've done, to get to Solo, to get him to flight—I've done for her. I'm thinking of sending her a letter, the old-fashioned kind. Grail-mail Bruce calls it, and of course he does.

I could do it up right, retro-style, use a feather from this hawk. I know how.

One summer Ruth had me and Bethany gather the largest crow feathers from under the locust where the long black seedpods fell. A quilting experiment. She cut the quills, and we dipped the hollow tips in a jar of homemade ink. She had us write out the alphabet on muslin, one letter per six-inch square. The ends of our feathers scratched and dribbled, the letters bled, and we were a mess by the end—stained fingers and blue-streaked faces where she drew designs like runes—less war paint than witch sign. We shook the pods we'd gathered like rain sticks and we danced, three crazed fates cavorting in the bluehouse. That was a good day.

Maybe Bruce would like it, if I wrote to our daughter.

I just wish Solo would stop testing my patience and come home. I've invested far too much to lose my data now. I admit it, I've underestimated his will. He clearly has the capacity to plan and to harm. I built a beast—a thinking beast capable of complex processing—only to have him take off on some kind of Corvid Rumspringa, adolescent and monstrous.

Slouching. Bruce would say, I know he would. *Towards Bethlehem.*

Everything is mocking me. The hawk looks like a pheasant retrieved by a loyal hound. The lights strung all across the county (another cruel example) are aping joy. I hate this. Being Bruceless. I do, I miss my poet's rants and his quotes. I even miss how he loved me less because it was—he was—right to.

Mina needed him more.

That's how it is after a child is born. How it ought to be.

Chapter Six

A DEVELOPMENT OF CROWS

⌄

Dear Mina,

I'm not quite sure what I'm doing. This seems a little formal, not very me. Your grandmother Ruth wrote letters she never sent. She left them as a sort-of present I guess. I found them after you and your dad left, and I've been going through them pretty slowly. I don't have much else to do right now. I'm waiting.

We didn't really do Christmas when I was little. Small necessary gifts only. Clothing and books. A big breakfast the morning of. No church, no tree. We never decorated, but not because we were atheists. We weren't really anything.

I know our family isn't religious either, but I hope it's been different for you. That it hasn't felt like a punishment or something withheld. Candy, or love.

I want to give you something this year, something big. One of the crows—the very last hatched. Bear with me. I know that after you saw the little ones, you wanted nothing more to do with them. But I raised him for you, Mina. His name is Solo. I was thinking if I got him there, into the air, you'd understand. You'd see how remarkable you could be . . . together.

But something has happened. He's missing.

Please don't worry about him. I'm sure he'll come back soon, and I'll make sure to be here when he does. It may be that he got a little bit overwhelmed by the sky. It's possible he got turned around up there. And this is what I need to tell you Mina: Solo flew! Your bird is flying and he is immense and magnificent and whole—and he's missing. But I know he'll come home. He has to.

Your aunt Bethany used to say I didn't know how to be with people. Before your dad and you left, he said I was incapable of asking for help. Maybe they're both right. I can't regret my nature, but I do regret the time you and I have spent apart. These past months have been so strange. I'm caught between who I used to be and . . . well, even before you went away, I wasn't feeling like myself. That's a weird phrase, isn't it? I mean—if I wasn't feeling like myself, who was I feeling like? I'm not sure I know how to answer that.

I stopped there. I was beginning to ramble, and I can't have her having that. Not from me.

⌄

Polaroid: *Agnes—age 12, Bethany—age 10*

R is taking more pictures. Blurs of life. She is mostly in the rocking chair in her room, mostly taking pictures of her daughters she asks them to dress for and dance in. There are clothes in the hope chest they have never seen before. Fancy and bad, mottled shades of blue . . . A and B are embarrassed by them. But their filigree buttons and slippery shininess seem to make R happy. They cannot deny her their twirling. As she rocks and sighs and rocks, they spin for her—they tornado.

⌄

Chapter Six

Dec14

Bethany came by today. She's never, not once before. Our visits have ever been one-direction affairs. Me-to-her.

She arrived just before noon.

I was clearing the dead rushes from beside the pond when I heard her pull up. I walked up the hill around the house to the driveway. She climbed down out of her mud-spattered pickup and stood wide, bracing. I know that stance. That and Pop's old peacoat, worn as hell, a loose button dangling.

That American made? I ask.

Don't do that.

Why are you here, Bethany?

She looked at me like Pop would, a slap he'd resist planting on your face, a stone rising from the pit of your throat, one you couldn't swallow if you wanted to—and you don't.

I see these crows you're breeding?

Not today, I don't think. Where're the kids?

They're home. Listen, Agnes . . . out near me, there's story of a black bird, size of an eagle, flying at night. Mechanic down in Gap, Josef Niemann, says he saw it. Tim heard him talking at the Tawny. He's been telling anyone who comes in every night for a week.

The Tawny Owl—a drunk mechanic's got you spooked?

Stop it.

In Gap, you say?

Between Paradise and Gap . . . off Slaymaker Hill Road.

Maybe double vision. That can happen to drinkers.

I'd had a sip this morning, hair of the dog. That plus physical labor bolstered my recovery from the bourbon that helped me sleep and when it didn't, didn't.

That bird one of yours?

How could it be, Bethany? Crow big as an eagle, it's not possible.

You said you were breeding them big—

Not possible. You know Halloween's been over, Sis.

They could be dangerous. They could swoop up chickens or bring down power lines. You shouldn't fool with such things, Agnes. You never could keep from messing with what God wrought— Arrogance in heart is an abomination to the Lord.

I'm afraid that I'm going to have to leave you alone with that horseshit.

I can't talk to you.

That's fine.

You contact Bruce lately?

What would I say to Bruce?

That a girl needs her mother.

Yep. I could say that. I could definitely say that. (I paused.) Did we though?

She turned and climbed back into the Chevy. She was still trying to clean up after. The effort she spent scrubbing three years of sick out of Ruth's room was beyond my understanding. That is, until Pop moved her out of the bed we'd shared since birth and into the room where our mother died.

From then on, he slept up in the attic with Ruth's things. I was alone. Alone and relieved. My mother had finally gone, let her be gone. He could die too, up there with her books and boxes—I'd have been fine with that.

When he did manage to die, I moved us back yes, but I avoided the attic for months. It was still their space. Then when we did go up, we cleared out most of Ort's junk but left hers untouched. It was only after Bruce left that I began to dole out the remnants of my mother's disordered thinking to myself.

I don't know if Pop decided to keep her diary from us, as he denied us most things, or if he hadn't bothered opening it, but this wasn't the day to tell my sister about Ruth's senseless scratchings.

I hope Solo flies where he will for as long as he will. Fuck Bethany. Fuck Josef Niemann. Let him mind his Kias and Toyotas, his Hyundais and Hondas. Despite protests to the contrary, besides trucks, no one around here buys American.

V

I had the dream again.

The first moment is always the phone call. Someone has reached out to interview me. The knowledge I have and they want has to do with flashpoints of different chemical compounds—at what temperature they will catch fire in the air. Suddenly I'm an authority on the subject. I do not immediately suspect the world is melting. This is the first sign.

> *How can we move forward after this?* the interviewer asks me.
>
> After what?
>
> *Excuse me. Are you no longer located outside of Philadelphia?*
>
> I am.
>
> *Look out your window.*

In the dream I live not in Kensington but in a tall apartment building with a view of the city, to the west, Ardmore or Narberth or Bala Cynwyd, and the sky is black. I note the fact of no stars. Dark smoke is moving quickly across the skyline. In a sudden siren blare, the city announces itself. Below the sky the world is a brew—sparking—seething with liquid red. It is on fire, all of it. The city is consuming itself in brimstone. Everything is awash in bloodlight. I see it for what it is: Hell.

I hang up the phone.

During the rest of the dream I am elated. This never changes no matter how many times I've had the dream. Bruce and I want to leave, we have wanted to leave, we are now leaving. We hate our jobs—mine with the company whose poisons passed through me into my daughter, his at the textbook publisher, copyediting propaganda. Because of the apocalypse out the window, these jobs no longer exist.

We can start over if we can manage to live. Fleeing will not be easy, but in the dream we are motivated. Survival is basic, simple—and simple is the root of joy. How have we forgotten this? Bruce starts filling containers with water. I throw clothes in trash bags and pull out an old tourist guidebook with roadmaps of the state parks. The internet, I assume but do not check, is down. I start plotting a shunpike route into the Poconos. We call no one. There is no point.

In the dream we never learn what has happened. We don't ask, we simply get to work. In the dream Mina is fenced in her play area to keep her from rolling into trouble. In the dream she is a toddler, not speaking, not asserting herself as she will later, telling me about all the things she can do that she cannot.

We go about our preparations but soon, exhausted by our busyness, Mina moans. I am never quick enough. Bruce snatches her up along with the scarf-sling he easily mastered and me, never.

Chapter Six

Back pain, I say in the dream and it was true in life, partly. I felt creaturely with a child pressed against my front body. Like we were primates. But that's not it, we *are* primates—more like she was an attached egg-clutch, like we belonged to some species of cannibalistic spider. My daughter was an already hatched thing but I didn't want to give her constant access to my body. Who would eat who first? Besides I shouldn't be so available to her, it would make her weak. I needed all the warmth I could generate and didn't want to share. At the same time, I know a child is nothing if not a furnace.

I think all these things one after another. Even in the dream I am aware they are feints. Lies.

Then I think—maybe *she* set the city on fire.

This is ridiculous: she is with us, has been. It must've been other people's children. Mina is calm now, wrapped into Bruce as we plot our escape from a dying world. She is his sedated sloth, his done-squirming hairshirt.

I don't want to leave her behind, that's not it. I want us all to make it, but I can't help wondering how long she'll be able to last in the mountains without her father. Which means I think it likely he will eventually sacrifice himself so she can go on. And—if I am forced to extrapolate—that I will not so sacrifice.

I don't ever go deeper than that in the dream. I don't ask myself whether I would pick her writhing body off his dead one and keep walking. I know this is the next question. I don't ask it. I want her to live but not to need me. I could be dead by that time too. That is the other potential I am aware of in the dream, the better one.

I couldn't get back to sleep after that. So I read.

V

DAUGHTERS,

Today, Bethany, you told me you hate living on a farm. You hate cleaning and mending and you hate school and you wish you were a fish and could swim away but, please believe me, you would be missed if you left. By your father too.

Did you two know I had a great-uncle Hop who rode the rails? My mother said he always talked about the ocean, but then he'd go see it and come directly back because the water there is too much like a sky, one you could drown in. I have never been, but I imagine it sometimes, when it storms.

This place may seem not big, not fierce, its land divided and subdivided into farms and towns with only small stretches of pines and sycamores along mill-tamed creeks—but the wild is still here. You can find it on treed ridges, in stagnant water in tractor ruts, where meadows have grown from fallow fields, among sumacs and ferns sprung up inside abandoned, roofless barns where your school friends will eventually go, like I did, to do all the shouldn't things. This place may seem tame to you now but that's just summer-thinking, and no weather lasts.

People once left other places to come here. They meant to escape hatred, but I think you cannot help but bring yourself wherever you go. According to schoolbooks, Quakers settled Pennsylvania—pacifist slave-trading Quakers arrived from Barbados (the schoolbooks don't tell you that)—as well as Anabaptists, Lutherans, German Reformed, Moravians, Rosacrucians. My own family was Catholic. So hypocrites and zealots of all stripes landed here, including powwowers, who practiced the folk healing they brought from Europe. Only their name is related to Native Americans, and that is stolen and misattributed, per usual. They called themselves Brauche or Braucherei, but others called it powwowing because they danced and SANG SONGS *in the woods, which is French for* BLOOD LIES *and, also, because if they were called witches something would've had to be done, and this was pacifist country.*

We knew people had come to Oma for her salves and charms. *A con*, Pop told us. *If they got better, it was her work, and if they kept hurting, God had reasons they should suffer*. She died soon after Pop came home from Vietnam, her prayers answered and him, whole. Ruth said a mother should've known better. Near her own end, she wanted Bethany and me to divulge our fears to her, all our hates and hurts. She swore if we talked she'd be there, she'd listen. But we knew by then—and we knew she knew—she would not.

⌄

DEC15

Solo must have been watching me. Must've seen Bethany when she came by and followed her home. He was there today when she went to start dinner. Tim called. *Your sister is babbling*, he said. He did not say, *My wife*. Could I come? He doesn't know who else to call, not the church, they'd try to exercise her. He said *exercise*. Their congregation believes in that shit, speaking-in-tongues and demons and the spirit-sculpting rites of jazzercize.

Shut up Agnes.

I am a terrible person. *The children are upset*, he said. *And Bethany won't do anything*. Not cook, not clean. Not nothing.

Tim's no star either.

⌄

I got Bethany into bed finally. More than an hour she sat there, at the kitchen table, muttering at the window.

It was there by the gate. It was just getting dark and it was beside the gate.

That's how I could tell it wasn't my eyes making it big—because of the gate—how it brushed against it, then shook its wing out like it was caught. It looked at me. Directly into me. Through the window like the window wasn't there, like it could reach me from there at the gate, like there was nothing to stop it.

You mean Solo.

And I knew it, I knew it. I threw my hands over my ears then because no. How is it possible, all of them in one body, you put them all into one body, Agnes, how could you? Did you marvel—because what-was and was-not has now come? How could you be so stupid?

Bethany, you need to lie down.

How did you not know you've been lied to? How can you think that it's you making these decisions? That you ever did? You vain idiot. You've always been blind. Books? Math? Pride! You're not in control. If you think you are, that's you—being controlled.

You're not making sense.

You're a puppet. They are up inside you jerking you around like a two-dollar whore.

A two-dollar whore. Really, Bethany, what century are you in?

Listen to me, Agnes. You have to kill it now. Kill it.

Solo.

Shush. Be quiet. You can't name it, don't give them a name. You give them a name, you're calling them to you, inviting them in.

So Solo's a vampire now?

*You think your cleverness will save you? It won't. You have brought evil here. To my door, my children's *home.* It was at the gate. Why did you ever, ever decide to come back here?*

Bethany you know why. Because Pop . . . and for Mina.

That's a lie. You wanted to show Bruce who you were so he'd leave you, and he did. And he took her. What did you expect him to do when he found out? People aren't perfect, Agnes.

Oh, I am aware.

They're sinners. You're a sinner.

But Bruce is a saint?

If he is, you drove him away for it. And why? To replace him with this? I felt it Agnes, cold and dark and swole like the Susquehanna in March. Why won't you face facts?

You don't truck in facts Bethany.

Tell me you don't remember our crows.

What about them?

*You listened to them. Do you not remember? Because I do. I remember you under the tree. They spoke to all us women, but you *listened.* Do you remember what they told you to do? Because I remember, Agnes.*

I remember helping you.

Once I got Bethany quieted and into bed, Canon and Prosper came out to the living room. Tim talked softly, pulling them close. Honor was singing to Forbes and Serenity, some hymnlike thing wafting down the hall. After a bit, Merit appeared out of the dark in a soft green nightgown. She tiptoed over to me and leaned forward to whisper: *Mommy loves you*. Her eyes were rimmed with lashes dark like Ruth's. She put her hand up to my face in that old-person way some children have. She is their most pensive. She looked like a paler, softer version of my daughter, come to comfort me. Of course, Mina has never done this—she doesn't really walk. I got up, went to the sink, and poured myself a glass of water I wished were bourbon. Tim sent his daughter back to bed. I took a few sips, said goodbye to Tim and the boys, and went home.

∨

DEC16

This time he left me a spine.

I think a groundhog's (~*Marmota monax*). This, based on the shape and length of the coccyx. I walked out to the pen at dawn, to see if he'd come home after scaring my sister shitless. The cold snap's over, snow melting. No bird, but in the muddy pen there was a snake of bones. Vertebrae, with bloody viscera hanging from them like fringe and beads.

Avian predation is not as well documented as you'd think, given the thousands of years humans have spent observing them, but there are isolated reports of birds of prey feeding this way: first severing a rodent's spinal cord, then seizing the base of the tail with their beaks as they stand on the body. One swift yank and the inside is out.

Though Solo's no raptor.

Beside the offering was something else catching the early light—like a flashlight skimming the surface of a mirror, broadcasting midnight trespass to passersby. I opened the gate. I made out a crystal pendant, its chain snapped, blackish, coated in half-congealed blood. Potentially the rodent's.

Wild crows have been known to engage in relationships with humans that last years. They bring items to curry favor with their people. Shiny things: coins and pins, bottlecaps and tabs from soda cans. Jewelry. This bit of glitz was not in and of itself an untypical Corvid gift.

The biomatter read more like a mafia threat: *This could be you*. But that's human logic at work—my own flawed thinking. Correlation does not equal causation. Or motive. Organized crime requires at least semiorganized thought. Solo's smart but not as smart as even a stupid mobster. Animals do threaten each other with demonstrations of size and power, but these occur only during real-time altercations.

Animals do not play chess.

The message confused me. No matter what he meant or didn't mean, the spine *felt* like a warning, but the necklace? That surely conveyed our bond—a find that reminded Solo of me, to come back to me. A nod to the strength of our relationship, a forget-me-not. It might explain him at Bethany's: something prompted him to follow her home, some curiosity about our sisterhood or jealousy of it. He may have sensed our tension. It's possible he feels she's a threat to me.

Alternately, these items could be trophies from separate kills.

Don't be ridiculous Agnes. A crow does not murder. A murder comprises more than one crow—by definition. Solo cannot in and of himself a murder make.

Where was Bruce when she needed language to save her? I ask myself. But poor Agnes, I cannot find her way to an answer.

V

Letter, cont.

. . .

What is important to remember Mina, is that he flew. Solo flew. I did that for you.

And I need you to know this: his first climb into the air—your bird's first skimming of sky—is a thing I will never be sorry for witnessing. No matter what else. How I wish you'd been with me then . . . for that first flight. Absolutely yes. I just wish that, to have been there, you did not have to first be in my womb.

I maybe shouldn't have written that. Your aunt Bethany says I'm cruel. But you need to know unwanted children don't suddenly wake up and want their own. At least, I didn't. Your dad and I took precautions against you . . . my insistence. Still, once I learned I was in fact pregnant, I want you to know I tried to imagine it—motherhood. I tried to picture a different labyrinth than the one I'd known. One without a cipher at the center. You have to understand, Ruth had provided me no working model, no prototype.

I wasn't even aware of you at first, not for months, long after I dropped the beaker. I'd been irregular since I first menstruated at twelve, so I paid no attention to that missed period, or the next. By the third one I felt something—fatigue, shortness of breath. I wasn't handling my alcohol as well.

I peed on the stick. I know it sounds like a joke but it's not, it's what you do. I bought the test at the drugstore near work and took it at lunch. I wanted to doubt it, but I knew how the mechanism worked. False negatives happen all the time, but if you can follow basic directions, false positives are vanishingly rare.

I told your father about you that night. He was beside himself. He spun me around like a top then freaked out and set me on the couch like a first edition. He wanted you and I wanted him to have what he wanted. So I stopped smoking and drinking—immediately and for the most part. Before I was showing I sometimes stopped after work at the bar six blocks from our apartment, but only for one drink and, if pressed, a second double. Strength to face your father's joy. You must know it by now, its unmeetable expectations.

I ask you—What kind of quality is that for a poet to lay claim to?

By the time I began showing, the veins in my chest pulsing blue, it was the end of month five. I began noticing puritanical looks from the happy-hour crowd. The bartender commented once. You sure?

Fuck him. Fuck Joey-fucking-Pavlic.

Apologies. I grew up in a place where cursing is a sin, where mirrors are small because of vanity, and photos rumored to steal your soul—judgment is in the water here. So I bought an emergency fifth. I stashed it at the bottom of the linen closet behind the folded-up tarp your father spread over the hardwood while he painted the office into a nursery.

> Sage green, *he said.*
>
> *Hospital-gown color, I thought. Institutional. Corpse skin.*
>
> *He said* soothing.

I let things drop back then. Because I loved him.

That's it for now. My hand is cramping, plus I just wrote a lie, or something close to one, and I don't want to do that. I won't. I'm beginning to hate Bruce. For starting this whole shitshow, for insisting that he loved me. For loving me. And that's not even it quite—if I hate him, it's only for loving Mina more . . . but I don't mean more than me. I mean more than I am able.

V

DEC16 (2 P.M.)

The emergency siren went off. My first thought was—tornado? In December? I turned on the radio. Not weather, they found Scylla Durfee's dress. Bloody rags in a cornfield.

Dogs have been brought in, a search organized.

The body has not yet been recovered. The announcer stuttered over the next part: *Given the state of the clothing and amount of blood at the scene, the sheriff's office suspects the inter—the interference of an animal. Or animals.* He asked the listening audience to report any abnormal behavior to the authorities, but not to approach, or shoot. He segued immediately back to high school basketball. After a minute or two it was as if he hadn't read the bit about the missing girl, her bloody goddamned dress. Manheim Central had trounced Penn Manor the night before: an alum, he felt compelled to gloat.

Probability points to Solo. He makes the most sense. We don't see bears near here much. They prefer deeper woods. Ours are sparse, small stretches between corn and bean fields and along the cricks. The few coyotes keep to themselves except for the howling. You see them dead on the interstate occasionally or limping along fences at twilight bald as chupacabras—when they've got the mange.

I suppose a pack might drag away and eat an already-dead girl if they were hungry enough. Dead girls do happen.

They happen less often out in the open though—right Agnes? But maybe I'm thinking of the missing ones who aren't dead. The ones kept in cellars and crawlspaces for years, sometimes by their own fathers, men who make Pop seem godly. Ort Krahn, the tragic but harmless widower-saint.

Chapter Six

Maybe when you kill a girl outright, without human shame, maybe out in the open would be a fine place to leave her.

⌄

To distract myself, I turned back to Ruth . . . not my best decision.

> *I tell you,* DAUGHTERS, *they say pacifist, they say no violence. They say violence was never welcome in this place when what they mean is violence done outside the home. Inside violence has another name: discipline. Discipline is tolerated as a form of baptism, of cleansing, and this is why we have mudrooms, and why we hang our brooms there, and belts, and when I was young, that is where we stood the switches.*
>
> *Children, they believe, need sustained correction, and most especially girl children. But wilderness clear cut or beaten down comes up through cracks, it seeps into wells. And if you're not born white? Count on nothing they say.*
>
> *I first read about the Conestoga Massacre when I was twelve, the same time I was learning how wild I was and would not be, not under my father's roof. In 1763, the Paxton Boys rode down from Harrisburg, come to exterminate the last few members of the Conestoga tribe. The militia were men who "in private life are virtuous and respectable" and who insisted that their crimes, "shall be considered as one of those ebullitions of wrath, caused by momentary excitement, to which human infirmity is subjected."* I don't expect you to read all my books, but I do need you to read enough to know that you are capable of transformation into something brutal, brutal and keen.*
>
> *Six people were slaughtered in their homes, and then fourteen more, including eight small children, hunted down after being taken into custody in Lancaster and there, under protection of the law, hacked to pieces. Most numbers, when divided by the limbs of children, quickly become infinite.*

For the monsters who hide in and among us, this is a sacred geometry.

Because the Conestoga were Christian and because they were "good" Indians with English names who traded with local Europeans, the massacre offended higher-minded colonists, men like Benjamin Franklin, who wrote this strongly worded nothing:

[And here, Ruth had pasted a passage excised from some book, its fuzzed straight edge betraying her use of a ruler.]

*"The barbarous Men who committed the atrocious Fact, in Defiance of Government, of all Laws human and divine, and to the eternal Disgrace of their Country and Colour, then mounted their Horses, huzza'd in Triumph, as if they had gained a Victory, and rode off—unmolested!"***

These men (and you can call them that, because land and butchery are among the most common preoccupations of men)—these men were never identified. And they never met the justice their neighbors claimed so publicly to desire.

The word Conestoga as you know it is not the name of a people so much as a marketing tool, a mobile symbol of MANIFEST DESTINY, *a phrase that hides mass murder between the folded rhyme of two words. I want you to think about that, about the music of words and what it covers over, how these great wheels and white sails roll over and over and over the dead, oceans of prairie crossed without thought, the sunken world.*

I wish I could ask Ruth—What is it I'm covering over?

There is an exact chemistry that makes up Solo's genetic code. From the top down, I've always thought the structure of DNA, as it is drawn in textbooks, resembled Pop's rototiller. Form fomenting function. I thought of how its spiral blades could be doing violence to the earth right now, if you thought of the earth as a girl, or a girl as the earth.

Chapter Six

I had done this. Loosed a violence. Introduced an invasive species to a landscape not mine to sow. I was born here, raised here, but all I've ever felt for here was hate: white sheets of hate I fastened over hoops to carry me away, black plumes of it poisoning a sky I saw more as my limit than any horizon.

* Words of the Reverend John Elder, leader of the group, in defense of the Paxton Boys' "Conestoga Massacre," as quoted by William Buell Sprague in *Annals of the American Pulpit: Presbyterian* (1859).

** From Benjamin Franklin's "A Narrative of the Late Massacres, in Lancaster County, of a Number of Indians, Friends of this Province, by Persons Unknown With Some Observations on the Same," (Philadelphia, 1764).

v

Before they found the dress, there was at least the possibility that Scylla had run away from her parents' Farmville fantasy. Because she missed the city, her friends, her Montessori school, because someone had yelled at her or raised their hand or taken off their belt.

Admittedly, at six, this wasn't as likely as it might be at, say, ten or twelve.

I don't know why I never tried escape. Finding my way to something different hadn't seemed possible somehow. School was what I had. It wasn't a good school and I had no friends: we weren't allowed them. Still—bullied, ignored, avoided—it was a relief to go, to spend the day away from Pop and Ruth. His cold, her strange.

Mina says she likes hers, that she's doing well. We didn't send her to the public here, I was sure it wouldn't work. We moved back in winter, halfway through the year. Still, Bruce wanted to visit. He spent one afternoon at my old elementary and we were, for once, agreed. Apparently, though, it wasn't the curriculum but the looks he and Mina got that convinced him. He wouldn't say more. *You'll ask if I'm sure I saw what I saw, and every time you do that, it literally takes me weeks . . .* He didn't finish. So we homeschooled. I mean he did—I wouldn't know where to start. So many of my PhD cohort wanted to run their own labs, train disciples, profess. That wasn't me. I never wanted to be in charge of people. Too many variables, irrational energies I'd be expected to first register and then negotiate.

I never loved school, I was just good at it. My sister, not so much. But Bethany was a model citizen—erasing boards, banging erasers, rowing-up rows of desks. Her nickname for years was Jan, short for janitor and also a reference to the Brady girl our classmates knew from reruns. We didn't have a TV. There was so much that kept us from getting along.

The two of us were slightly-off versions of the same odd: same blotchy blue dresses, same haughty shyness and speech, stuttery and stilted. So we hid. Bethany would act the teacher's aide at lunchtime, and I'd head to the library or the science lab to talk with Mr. Walsh about colors of flame.

Why do you come here?

He asked me that once we'd exhausted all he knew. I told him, I think I'm repulsive. When he tried to reassure me, awkwardly, I told him no—I meant the physical property, like in an electron pair. I think it would be best, I said, if I situate myself far from other students.

He tried not to laugh at that, failed.

Bruce has told me I can be, at times, inadvertently funny. In Philly when I accidentally made a joke, he and Mina would erupt, his deep laugh echoing from the corners of her tiny body. I liked the sound, even if I wasn't inside of it.

Chapter Six

My sister was small like that—like my daughter. So small that on our bus rides home she slid across the seat, bumping my hip at every left. To avoid this, I'd pull her in. We'd nap like that, shutting out the other kids. Her breathing was quick and shallow and I'd close my eyes listening to it until the bus driver yelled our name: Krahn. It was good we slept, or pretended to. We had to rest up for chores.

After we'd eaten and cleared away dinner, Pop walked us around house and yard to check off our daily list. We stood as close to military-grade attention as we could muster, and he surveyed. Inevitably, he'd shake his head before painstakingly repeating whatever task we thought we'd done. This process could go on well past dusk. Us, struggling to stay upright at five and seven, eight and ten, nine and eleven. Him, fixing our failings.

The first time we were instructed to weed Ruth's kitchen garden, we were little. It was caged, and the cage leaned in like it would like to eat us. The jagged wire was meant to keep out rabbits and deer, but even picking tomatoes from there scared us. It was like a mouth. A footpath of flat stones made a toothy loop through the peas, cucumbers, squash, and another semicircle through the peppers, tomatoes, and herbs in their patch at the far end, nearer what Ruth called the bluehouse. It took us hours that first time—to weed, to floss.

Pop examined our work one square foot at a time. At every half-pulled root, he unfolded his body and strode over to us up against the screen door. There was a lightbulb above us, also caged. It was late, and moths flitted by our faces. We knew better than to bat at them. He bent in half, again, to hold what he'd wrenched up under our noses.

He was trembling. Veins stood out on his thick forearm, his face redder than from the sun, stippled with the salt of beard shadow, his breath earth-peppery as a radish. This was Pop, straining not to grind wild scallions into our faces. The bulbs reeked. They were so hard to wrest from dry earth, we couldn't. We hadn't. We shook.

This was another kind of school.

Pop had an odor, an open red smell, like blood not yet dried. Like the spot where a yanked tooth was, sore and oozing. My father was one long threat, from straw hat to resoled boot. The fact that he never struck me maddens me beyond telling.

Except I did tell. I told the crows.

⌄

B: Ness—

A: I didn't know who else to call.

B: What is it?

A: I think I may have hurt someone.

B: What?

A: Not me, I think one of the birds hurt someone.

B: They got out?

A: There's only the one now.

B: It attacked? Who? How bad is it?

A:

B: Nessie? Are you there?

A: Bruce, it's all my fault.

B: What are you talking about?

A: I think she's dead.

Chapter Seven

A CONFIDENCE OF CROWS

⌄

DEC17

Bruce is on his way. Mina will stay with his parents.

I've been out looking for Solo. I need to bring him back to the barn. I've been listening to the radio on scan. Just a few seconds on each station to check for sightings. None yet.

Or maybe one.

I heard half a verse of *Lay Down Sally*, a partial weather forecast (freezing rain), a religious station preaching the degradation that comes from trusting in your own moral compass, a scratchy report on Baltimore football. And, two nights ago in Gettysburg, a UFO: a dark silent glider. The bonfire-goers who called in thought it a tricked-out drone—convinced they'd smelled a chemtrail.

I have Ruth's ornithology book with me. I'm at a Wendy's looking at it, bought a Frosty so I could sit. I'm checking the local roosts from the past century and a half. The largest gatherings of Solo's ancestors were reported along the Susquehanna but some were further south and west, closer to York, though none as far as Gettysburg.

I can't get the midnight drone out of my head. There's also this number: fifty thousand deaths in three days on that battleground.

I'm wondering now how that number equates to gallons of blood, and if Solo could've followed the scent of century-and-a-half-old carnage. People seem able to.

I went on four school fieldtrips to Gettysburg. I keep seeing the crow there. I'd call it intuition if I believed. I don't. Pop told us the glorification of war was worse than wrong, it was dangerous, but he never kept Bethany or me off the bus, and when Ruth couldn't, he signed the permission slips. Wet green hills, a treeline edged with boulders called the Slaughter Pen, the slope of Pickett's Charge: reenactors always there wandering the grounds—middle-aged men loading cannons and attaching bayonets to the ends of rifles. It wasn't until we were on a tour with a class of kids from Reading that I noticed the players' overwhelming whiteness. There were no women either, acting the soldier. Just a few Pitcher- and Nightingale-types behind the lines, dressed more for slinging ale than dressing wounds.

War fantasy has always confused me. I was pretty sure all soldiers came back like Pop, harder and wronger, that everyone knew that.

There's a man two tables away from me with muttonchops, scarfing down his square burger like it's the end times. I bet I know where he spends his weekends, but he's not at it today—his cap isn't blue or gray, it's red.

There's a topographical map in Ruth's bird book, color-coated in eight kinds of yellows and magentas. I think first I'll head to Chiquesalunga—Chickie's Rock. From the ledge I'll be able to see up and down the river. Before the Civil War battle, Union scouts hiked up the ridge to watch for the Rebels' approach. This I learned on an entirely different fieldtrip. There used to be a trolley that brought people up to a ridgetop amusement park there. A gazebo near the overlook commemorated the spot where a Native American Juliet threw herself to her death after her English Romeo was killed for courting her. That tragedy occurred two and a half centuries before

Lincoln delivered his three-minute soliloquy down the road. Our tour guide that day was a hyperanimated woman with turquoise glasses who flushed with each new story of miner, soldier, lover, or fatal trolley accident caused by—get this—potato bugs. A bumper crop of their dead bodies found vengeance against the machine that killed them, the tracks made slick with their insides.

Some places are, as Ruth noted, historically crowded.

Muttonchops just smiled at me and touched the brim of his cap. I've been staring. He looks like a man willing to help a girl in need. I should put up some fucking fliers.

LOST, LARGE CROW!

ANSWERS TO "SOLO." DO NOT APPROACH.

Goddamn it. Solo's gonna be shot.

There's too much stupid around here—dozens who'd kill the bird as soon as look at him, and all of them own guns. Because fear. Because of his size. His color. Because crows have a bad rep among farmers who don't call their human effigies scare-thrush, for fuck's sake. I need to find him before someone else does.

But if he killed the girl? If Solo would come back to the barn, I could figure things out. The bird likely has no conceptual understanding of what he's done.

During my dozen years at DDR, I was on a team hired to repurpose compounds originally designed for war. We tweaked the recipes toward absorption, so that these chemicals could "eat" other chemicals out of the atmosphere. The work was described to me as essential. I was working to forestall global warming they said, and I chose to believe them, all the while knowing any trials would be done in the sky above oceans or developing nations—this, to minimize human fallout. Minimize. I didn't press for details. Instead I custom-designed their poisons.

I told myself I didn't need an excuse: I was good at what I did, I got paid for it, and well. The factory assigned me to a room and in I went. Scalding or Slitting. Evisceration.

At DDR they called it Re-synth.

I'm beginning to think Solo knows more than I've imagined. That maybe he has his own reasons. The bird looks like a judge—I've always thought so. That he may be here as executioner is not such a horrible thought. If only he would limit his justice to me.

Muttonchops is gone. On his way out he dropped his number at my table with a note written on ripped piece of fry-box:

You look like a good time. And I know how to have one.

My Frosty's melted a bit—still that strange gray-brown color. If the sky were this color people would be frightened. There'd be a thousand news articles, protests blocking traffic in major cities, texts to elected officials.

And then we'd get used to it.

V

I got lost. Climbing.

I don't mean lost. The path is wide. From the road where I parked, it's not much more than a mile to the ledge, if that. I mean I lost my sense of things. Of what I was doing there.

I felt led.

The hawks were multiple. The name for a group of hawks together, circling above some dying thing, is a boil. There was a boil of hawks at Chickie's Rock. They floated at eye level with me. We were far above the river, above the train tracks that run along the river.

We all were there, and the wind.

Chapter Seven

The train is why the Confederates came to Pennsylvania in 1864. They meant to cut the Union supply line. This is what I was taught, in school and at Gettysburg, but up in the attic among Ruth's books I learned more about their tactics. In the weeks before the battle, raiding parties had come across the Mason-Dixon Line and grabbed free Blacks to sell into slavery. Hundreds of people kidnapped from their homes and farms. Hundreds of others fled to Philadelphia and New York, never to return. The region, blanched.

It's a strategy rarely discussed in textbooks, terror as prelude. I can't imagine that fear—not of death, that one's all around—but of being disappeared, made gone. Never-mattered.

This kind of erasure embrittles battle, stops the river that flows into battle and carries blood away, though never all the blood. Some blood goes into the soil. Some makes it into the groundwater. Some blood we drink later as water—limestone-strained and devoid of its original reason for being shed. Some blood brings crows.

The thing on the tracks was a small thing. I saw the first hawk plummet, then snatch, then carry its prey to a nest on the ledge. The small legs dangling from the hawk's beak moved not from its life, extinguished, but from air currents formed by its killer's flight.

Solo will go after what is easy to go after. A rodent. A girl. What matters less? This is the nature of a crow: to be smart about things. To conserve energy, to think three (but not seven) steps ahead. A crow cannot play chess. A crow can make fear, but not plot it out.

I'll find Solo, I have to.

V

DEC18 (5 A.M.)

Bruce is in my childhood room—Mina's until he took her from me. I found him in the kitchen when I got back. He'd brought me a salad from a diner off 83.

I had them put steak on top.

Why?

I was guessing your past few months have been heavily canned. I'm right, you're thin.

How was your drive? Is that your mom's car? Are you sure your parents are okay with Mina? Why did you come?

Fine. Yeah, smells like her post-trial cloves. I'm sure. You asked me.

I did.

You did.

We ate, at least I tried to. His salad was Greek, but with canned black olives and not the kalamatas I knew he'd ordered it for. He squinted, then sniffed and made a face. I explained about the potatoes, how their odor had stayed on, how it kept lingering.

Did you say . . . fingerling?

He smiled and I ignored it. I started to tell him about Scylla, the girl gone missing, but he'd heard all about it on the news on his way up. We sat across the kitchen table from each other. The fireplace gaped. When we'd first arrived, Bruce had tried to cook in it and smoked up the place. He had the flue cleaned, a bigger job than we'd budgeted. It had been filled with debris, and at least one desiccated squirrel carcass. The house was old, some of its bones more obviously disintegrating.

Chapter Seven

And you think the bird did this?

Solo? I do.

He stared hard at me.

You didn't name the others. You told me that was a problem, if you started to do that, that would be the sign of a problem.

You named me, Bruce. Was that our problem?

I hadn't meant to do this. This was not the time. But here he was, back in the house. Why shouldn't he answer for leaving?

You mean Nessie?

The name he gave me is a common-enough nickname for Agnes. But there are others. Bethany had called me Ag when we were teenagers. In grad school, I sent a couple poems into the university's literary magazine. A phase—but I signed them Silver. No one got the joke, which requires a passing knowledge of the periodic table.

I tried to explain it to Miss Deb and she laughed: *You're a hoot. Why wouldn't you want credit for your own words?* I lived in her house for seven years, we were familiar but not family. *Silver's no name for an educated woman, you might as well call yourself Tinsel. Or Trinket.* Her lectures were more animated than my professors'—I enjoyed them. By the end of our time together, I was hauling her trash to the curb, shoveling snow, and sitting with her at breakfast where I helped monitor her daily medications, Band-Aids really, applied too late to too large wounds.

Bruce looked at me across the table.

You like Nessie. You like having a name that isn't from here. You told me that.

Miss Deb had her own children—a daughter she wouldn't speak of and a son-done-good but out of state. When she died, he sold the rowhome where I'd spent three undergrad years and four more during my doctorate. Clayton was in software in North Carolina and never liked the idea of me, kept telling her she should raise my rent. He'd fly Miss Deb down every Easter. Twice, we'd gone hat shopping in preparation. She liked them big and swoopy and could pull that off. The first year she made me buy myself a gray pillbox—*for your inner Jackie*—which I couldn't. The following spring, she took me to a consignment store on Lancaster and I found a dress.

> I do. Or . . . I did. But it's not me. If you want a divorce, it won't be from Nessie.

I was wearing it when Bruce and I met—a vintage navy crepe sheath with a high neck and a rusting zipper. My poet-dress, though I was already a chemist by then, working toward my PhD in a lab on campus. I'd seen a flier: fancy book launch for a chaired professor. The idiot had padded the audience by inviting two talented grad students to read with him, a major concept error for someone who sounded like a bot.

Bruce read four poems—two rage-adjacent and two oddly tender.

Free, stolen anyway, we're over-
due to libraries gone
digital, gone homeless.

He went short. I later learned poets don't do that. I remember thinking at the time that no one should have a voice like his and not get paid for speaking.

Mist on a dark pond at dawn.

After we'd been dating a month I asked him, Why Nessie? And he said, *You hide from everyone, that plus you have a long and sexy neck.* And then he leaned over and kissed it.

On one of her loose graph pages Ruth wrote my given name, strung together, over and over. It's supposed to mean *pure* or *holy*, even *lamb*. But all I could make out was *anger* and something like *strange*, the loop on the *g* hanging down below the lines of text in dropped stitch.

After I heard Bruce read, I never wrote another poem. She would have liked him.

Miss Deb, I mean.

⌄

Polaroid—*a deep blue sky with a single cloud, tinged orange.*

This photo is taped inside the diary, Ruth's blue scrawl beneath—

Daughters,

> *Your father says all my flowers have died. That man does not mince truth.*
>
> *It was back during my brief time at college that I began my research on natural indigo. A waste of time, provincial, adolescent: these were the words leveled at me during my second-year critique. I did not return.*
>
> *Before I left, I learned about Eliza Pinckney, a woman who grew up on a Caribbean plantation called Poorest and, in 1738, began managing one of her father's South Carolina holdings. Rice. Agnes, if I tell you she was my Curie, you may have some idea. Eliza was sixteen when she assumed her managerial duties, not much younger than I was when I met her at the Free Library on the Parkway. I'd just finished reading Goethe and Albers on color and taken the train into Philadelphia, after I realized I could not wait up to three weeks, a ridiculous period to wait for an interlibrary loan.*
>
> *I was nervous to be in the city, but this was not the Philadelphia Jeannie warned me about. My roommate enjoyed her fear, the feeling of keys she showed me how to splay between knuckles. But*

I walked unmolested from 30th Street Station to the library on my mission to find out about indigo—the color, not the plant. After a few hours, I began to understand how botany, slavery, paint, marriage, pink blossoms, warmer woad—everything—is part of everything.

That day I saw more black people than I had in my life before then. There was the one French girl, Monique, in my drawing class—elegant beyond any attempt at speaking to. The librarian who helped me was black. She pointed me to Eliza's journal. I learned that day how indigofera was introduced to American fields by extracting knowledge from West African farmers, and that extraction is a large part of the history of blue gold, a nickname to baffle a colorist's mind.

I remembered then that Ruth used to mix up our names, Bethany's and mine. That she'd sometimes called one of us Eliza, usually me, and the other Polly, and I'd never had any idea why.

v

(6:30 A.M.)

Bruce still isn't up. I suppose travel can wreck you, same as stuckness. When he and Mina were thinking of taking the greenhouse on as a project, he asked me what we'd grown there. I told him, indigo. So many varieties of that plant—French, Japanese, Guatemalan—pink blossoms and compound leaves. Ruth grew other flowers for a few seasons and sold them to a local roadside market that also took Pop's blueberries, his sweet corn and tomatoes. The bouquets didn't use up her time, not like the quilts. I remember her cutting and cording the flowers at the kitchen table when I was little and me not wanting Pop to take them out. I wanted to set them around the house in their buckets and pails. I wanted to make a magic forest. I wanted color. I never saw Ruth paint a single canvas though she often threatened to make us sit for a portrait. Then she'd laugh—and it was sunflowers. But it wasn't funny. It was the worst punishment either of us could imagine: me and my sister forced to spend our Ruth hours still and silent. Like our Pop hours. I was maybe seven when I learned the big glassy outside room was not really a bluehouse, as our mother referred to it. It stank of fish. Indigo thrives in nitrogen-rich soil and she fed her plants a homemade emulsion made from Pop's catches. Too-small trout and bass plus sawdust plus unsulfured molasses plus two weeks in a jar. He let me help sometimes if I didn't talk. He was the one who told me fertilizer could be used to make explosives and how in Vietnam he had buddies who fished with grenades. *No skill in that.* Not a nice thing to say about friends, I thought, though I had no point of reference.

∨

(11 P.M.)

Today was a long day. I thought Bruce understood. Yes, Solo may have done wrong, but now he's in danger.

Bruce wants to help me, but not in the way I need help.

Before we left this morning, I told my husband all the things he couldn't be bothered with when he was here. I explained Corvid behavior in general and this one's, specifically. I took him out to the pen and then the barn. I showed him the wall where Solo makes his marks.

How big is he?

Big.

How has no one seen him?

I didn't tell him Solo had been seen—by drunks and potheads and conspiracy theorists—that the crow had become a Rorschach test for the reality-compromised.

He must be flying at night.

This was the only explanation I had and it seemed true, but it wasn't typical. Crows sleep at night. But I'd used heat lamps and hormones to condense my birds' daily cycle for four generations. I'd sped up maturity, growth, breeding, everything—faster living through chemistry. All Corvids are smart, but Solo outperformed any known crow on every test I set him to. Maybe crow-life was not for him, I said to Bruce. Maybe he doesn't want to crow anymore.

He doesn't know anything else. Just here, just you.

I had wondered about this. Most crows, when they leave the nest, establish homes near their kin. Ones that travel farther seek areas similar to where they were raised. Urban crows stay urban. Rural crows avoid the city. Solo would be close, seeking out something familiar in the terrain, something that would remind him of this place. This is not what I said to Bruce.

Ruth had a book of old roosts near here. It's possible this information is embedded in his DNA.

Like salmon?

You do listen.

I've always listened, Ness. I just can't always follow. So. You're saying this crow may have access to ancestral memory.

Epigenetic memory . . . it's possible. I want to go to Gettysburg.

There're roosts there?

None that I'm aware of.

He looked puzzled. I didn't explain my theory about the blood.

Bruce had never been. He drove us there around noon. I looked out the window the whole hour drive, knowing I wouldn't see Solo, scanning the sky anyway—a blanket of gray wool—it hadn't yet begun to snow.

We stopped at the visitor's center. I remembered there were viewing towers but was unsure where. We picked up a map for the self-driven tour, which ranged around the town. Beside the battlefield, a privately owned "classroom in the sky" used to loom above the trees—an immense hyperboloid observation structure with a 360-degree view, an eyesore demolished at the turn of the millennium, a few years after my tenth-grade history teacher took us up to the top and a kid named Orrin Fink threw up because what else is there to do inside a life-sized diorama of death?

> *Your school took you up some random guy's vanity project?*
>
> It was educational. We learned about property rights. You *do* know they were a thing during the Civil War?
>
> *You're not funny.*
>
> Not usually.
>
> *My dad's people came up from coastal Georgia, right after. Farmers and fisherman.*
>
> I didn't know that.
>
> *Neither did he. Internet genealogy. Dad's revisiting his history, he says, for Mina's sake.*
>
> What does that mean?
>
> *Hell if I know. He used to brush off my questions.* You're here now, son—own that.

Three smaller towers were marked on the map, each a few stories tall: one on Culp's Hill, one on Longstreet, one at Oak Ridge. It was my plan to climb them, not so much to find Solo as to look around for a place he might be hiding.

The snow began to fall around 2 p.m. These were the big shaggy flakes Ruth called onion snow because they could be as big as that, slices of onion. Given the right conditions, snowflakes the size of dinner plates can form. I never caught one that large. Their ephemerality tends to frustrate climate scientists. They're forced to rely on amateur accounts from kids like the kid I was, prepping black construction paper in the freezer to carry out with rulers into the cold.

The temperature was dropping, the snow falling faster.

Ruth's memory was sound. Her problem was in how she put together what facts she collected. This was the same issue as with her quilts: each square perfectly dyed and stitched, only the piecing pattern egregious. Warped faces and figures hid among her colors—distorted. Pop told us she was mistaken about the snow, that onion snow falls in spring, after planting. It's the last snow of the season, light and gone too quickly. Uncatchable. *You're my onion snow*, he said to her at the end. I think I remember him saying that.

Bruce thought climbing towers in this weather was not advisable.

> *Explain this again to me.*
>
> I can't.
>
> *Just have a feeling? That's not you—to not have logic, not know why.*

Bruce came with me up the first metal tower, though he's bad with heights, then slipped on the way down, barely catching himself with an arm thrown over the railing. He did not attempt the next two, kept suggesting we head back to the house. The ground was white by this time, and it was hard to make out much through the precipitation. He made a good argument, the roads were slickening, but also—Solo would be easier to spot against the snow. We circled around the south end of the self-guided loop and parked at Little Round Top. There, I entered a memorial to two New York regiments that looked like a toy castle. The turret was closed so I could only get as far as the second level. It was high enough.

I looked out and I knew. I couldn't see him, but Solo was out there. I felt him, out in the trees beyond the rocks, watching us.

When I came down, Bruce saw I was upset.

> *What is it?*

I pointed down to a field of boulders I'd scrambled over long ago despite Mrs. Shrike's warnings of sprained ankles and sunning snakes. Devil's Den: a formation perfectly designed for hide-and-seek, climb-and-claim, duck-and-snipe.

> *What are you thinking?*
>
> That Solo is drawn to places of death.
>
> *Aren't all crows carrion eaters?*
>
> They are. I mean they do, they will—they're omnivores like us. But that's not . . . I think he's feeding on *old* deaths.

The snow made the footing on the hill uncertain and it was getting colder. It had been July, not December, when a few Confederate sharpshooters used the natural cover to drop hundreds. Returned shots rang against the rocks, deafening some, killing others in ricochet. I made my way, nearly falling twice, onto one of the largest boulders to see what I could. Bruce protested but followed.

Staring out into the trees to the west, I imagined myself at eighteen, myself as a boy with a rifle, in Vietnam, peering into the jungle from which my death—or the deaths I was destined to deliver—would emerge.

We stood there, flakes drifting down around and between us. I'd missed Bruce: this was undeniable. Being apart hurt, though I'd fought the feeling. There'd been distance for years, maybe since the beginning. I wanted to let Bruce and Mina go . . . since I clearly couldn't do what was required to keep them. They were each other's—not mine—and this caused an actual physical ache in me, worse than forgetting to eat. I'd done my best to blunt it with work, first at DDR and then in the barn. Now that they'd gone, the gnawing would pass, it would, I just needed to push through. Besides, the whole shitshow was inevitable . . . I should never have been with Bruce in the first place.

Miss Deb was sick when we started dating, and for months I delayed introductions. She kept saying I should bring him over, she wanted a look, how was this one going to understand what I did, hell, how was any man? But I knew. I knew she would meet him and love him and because he was Bruce, a beautiful Black man, a writer, a *poet*—and she'd pronounce that word with reverence—she would've known he wasn't for me. So I kept them separate. Then one morning I came into the kitchen, and she was on the floor, her green silk robe puddled on the tile around her as if she'd died from a fit of spring.

White is snow. Cold is distance.

I would try. I would try explaining my sense of things to him, though that sense has been admittedly kicked loose. My mind is not now the methodical mind I learned to count on early, and it hasn't been for some time. The connections I see now are harder to hold. There are sudden insights I'm forced to reverse-engineer the logics for, if I am to allow myself to trust them. I want to trust them.

To trust him.

> You know I raised the crows in Pop's barn. All of them, including Solo.

> *I do.*
>
> But he was different. His mother mated with his brother, and I didn't plan that, or—not the way it happened. Solo was sired by his older brother, moments before their mother killed him.
>
> *You told me, Ness, these aren't humans. They don't behave like people.*
>
> They don't behave like crows.

This had been haunting me since it happened. Solo's mother was damaged, her behavior so aberrant I had to end her. After that, I should've been watching her offspring more closely. Those traits can be passed down—hell, Solo's sister offed herself. I never should've unchained him, never let him out. He came back bloody and I ignored it. I lied to myself, worse even than falsifying data.

> *What do you mean?*
>
> Crows may on occasion engage in incest in the wild, but they don't kill their sons, or their mates. They aren't mantids.
>
> *But these aren't wild crows. You messed with them.*
>
> That's true. I sped up their metabolism. I enhanced their size, their intellect. I fed them drugs. Their days and nights were artificial. I clipped their wings.
>
> *Yes. You did that.*

To Bruce, science was a lab I holed up in to avoid living. To avoid mothering. To avoid myself. All he knew about my project at DDR was that it was technical and as-yet unapplied. I never told him what my chemicals did, or were likely to. Kill. That data was above my paygrade and I didn't ask to be privy to it. Besides, my husband couldn't imagine my work as either creative or destructive—it was math. I'd played around with the birds, sure, but this was to him genetic sudoku.

I tried another tack.

Do you know what a locust is?

Sure. A plague. One of Egypt's big ten . . . that, or any place with a cross.

What?

Locus—t.

He was making a plus-sign with his fingers. Smiling. Bruce's parents were the first atheists of their deeply Christian families. It united them. But for both Bruce and me, godlessness was a hand-me-down—we weren't truly invested in our heresies. It was just another lack we'd had in common.

Here I was, trying to let him in, and my husband was closing me down with a joke, a pun better made on paper. Fucking poets. Bruce used to go on about wanting to know what I was thinking, how I was thinking it, but he didn't really want to know. No. I scare him. He came when I called—shown up, I guess to try to save me—only he couldn't ever help himself: he was abandoning me. Again.

Why are you like that?

Like what? He looked wounded.

I'm sharing, like you always say you want, and you climb into your words. Scurry into a crack in some language wall.

This was not where I'd wanted to go. He reached over and took my hand. I was exhausted, I let him. My fingers burned. Night was falling fast. I looked out into the woods.

Sorry, Ness. It's a swarming insect, right?

I wanted to punish him, but I needed to answer, to say things out loud. Hearing my thoughts lately, or seeing them on paper, helps me identify which make sense. Since Solo's been gone, I've found myself speaking to no one—especially at night—or writing it out. Trying to. Unfortunately, much that seems solution at 3 a.m. precipitates out by morning, and I'm left in the dark in the dawn, my head pounding, whiskey or no.

> Actually, locusts are nothing more than a type of grasshopper . . .
>
> *Grasshoppers. I might've read that somewhere.*

I paused. I looked down at our hands. I could barely feel his.

> Yes, grasshoppers. Incited into another form by an uptick in serotonin. It transforms the solitary field jumper into one of ten thousand mouths inside a massive cloud of consumption.
>
> *So he *is* swarming?*

Bruce was smiling. Another joke—as if swarming could be singular. What was his game here?

> What I'm *saying* is that altering an animal's brain chemistry can affect not just its form but also its behavior. Profoundly. Do you know how you go about altering an animal's brain chemistry?
>
> *How?*
>
> By manipulating its environment.
>
> *You have to back up, I'm not following.*

My husband was not this dense. I turned to face him and we dropped hands. I was feeling a little unsteady but decided to answer him as if his questions were honest—not stabilizing agents for an unhinged ex. I pointed to the high ground we'd just left, then moved my hand across the horizon to the trees screening Solo from view as he evaluated Bruce.

I can only assume that was what the crow was doing.

> Animals are changed by their surroundings. Like words by their context. Take *fix* for example: it means to change for the better, except when it means to keep from changing.
>
> *Hold on.* Bruce lifted an eyebrow. *You telling me science *doesn't* make any more sense than poetry?*

I couldn't help myself, I laughed. He can still do that—and it's fucking unfair.

> No, it definitely does. But it's not all about the blueprints. Our bodies are the boss. Our DNA sends us messages, but so does trauma. Experiences can turn our genes on and off—through chemistry.
>
> *Mmm. That's not trifli—*

Something moved out across the clearing in the trees.

I went still, and Bruce followed my lead. A few tense seconds peering into nothing, then a dog burst out at the edge of the wood. A big one, a German shepherd, bounded through the snow followed a few moments later by a boy in a plaid coat. He called the dog to him—a long, low, eerie whistle. Funereal. The dog came and the boy slapped snow off his coat before noticing us. He waved and the dog barked, a bark of greeting, and the two headed north toward town. I turned back to Bruce.

> It's how we learn. And Corvids are intensely intelligent—self-aware even.
>
> *Now there's a claim.*
>
> What would you call it? They recognize themselves in mirrors, imitate human speech, multistep problem-solve. They cooperate. They create rich family structures where lazy uncles step up to help raise orphaned offspring. I created none of these traits, but I may have tweaked the recipe.
>
> *The recipe?*

> It's a metaphor, Bruce. You cook—I'm talking the mental broth the birds' minds were stewed in.
>
> *Clipping their wings changes the broth?*
>
> Not just that. (I paused, searching for another example.) Dogs.
>
> *Dogs?*

I gestured in the direction of the interlopers, now a joint smudge in the growing dark.

> Breeds are manufactured—over centuries, yes—same principle. Controlled mating, feeding, training. Solo's diet was rich in synthetic hormones and tryptophan, a serotonin precursor. That, plus social isolation, a lack of sunlight, no real access to nature: all of these factors together may have mixed to form a perfect . . . cocktail of neglect.
>
> *Neglect? You're shitting me, right?*

His tone had shifted.

> *Those birds were anything but neglected. You . . . you *slept* with them. You were never with us. Even when you were with us, you weren't with us.*

Jesus, he was actually pissed. Here he was, the man who'd left me, I saw it now—the weak bond. The whiner. Just because he was right didn't mean he wasn't missing my point. Which was Solo. Solo was what was important here.

I volleyed.

> I'm good at what I do. Excellent, in fact. I learned early, and can still perform, a hundred variations of neglect. But that doesn't matter . . .
>
> *How doesn't it?*

He was seething, I saw it. And then I saw him recognizing his anger and starting to push it down. Screw that. I needed to get this out.

> I think Solo's breeding stock must've been contaminated—by the bird whose nest we found in the barn. The one we never saw.

I was shaking, heart pounding. My hair was wet and my arms ached, but at least I'd tried. Solo was exceptional, Bruce needed to get that, to understand why he was, and that it was *my* fault. *My* responsibility. You can't begin an experiment with an unknown variable. I knew better. The science wasn't flawed, the scientist was.

I hadn't realized how shot I was—how little I'd slept in the past few days. Weeks really. When my knees buckled, Bruce helped me sit. We slid off the rock, him first, to help me down. He guided me slowly back up and over the hill toward the car. It had gotten dark in the past half-hour, and the Subaru was the only vehicle there. Even from a distance, even dizzy, I could see the body strewn across the hood.

A doe.

She was ripped open, a fawn leg protruding from her abdomen. A dark twig.

∨

Bruce made black beans and rice.

He'd pushed the carcass off the hood and rubbed off as much blood as he could with snow. I still felt weak. I rested in the passenger seat as he rushed through these steps. He kept glancing around. No one was there of course. Solo is smarter than that. In a few minutes we were heading back toward 30. The wipers had iced up and visibility was poor. Bruce had to concentrate on the road. I fell asleep.

Chapter Seven

I woke when we turned onto the gravel. We got inside, and he cooked us up two bowls. He asked how I was feeling.

Stronger. Though my limbs are a little jelly.

He laughed, despite everything. It was a phrase Mina used with him when they were doing her exercises. But then he tried to take a bite and couldn't. He put his fork down.

You're telling me a crow did that.

I am.

I was feeling a little giddy. Solo was still following me, keeping tabs on me. It should make him easier to catch, especially with Bruce's help. I had some hope.

That's insane.

It is. Worse than with Bethany.

What happened with Bethany?

He followed her to her house a few days ago. Shook her up pretty bad.

She saw the bird?

Yes, Bruce, she saw Solo. I think he was there trying to figure out our relationship—same way he was watching us today. I'm thinking the deer was him asserting dominance . . . maybe because you're a man. He didn't leave anything at my sister's.

I could tell he wanted to say something.

Unless you think you have some other explanation?

He didn't. Solo had just announced himself to Bruce, blatantly, had done me that small favor. I dug into my bowl. The beans were good—I always forget to add the cumin.

There's only one that makes any real sense.

There were actually two possibilities for Solo's presence at the battlefield. Either I was right about Gettysburg—that Solo was somehow drawn to its tang of death—or the bird was upset enough to be tracking me. Crows remember faces. Crows assign responsibility.

And what's that?

DDR. Someone wants you discredited, for good.

I stopped eating. This was out of nowhere and it was ridiculous. I'd had no contact with the company for three years. None. Bruce knew that.

It had been a long process, deciding to sue. The company's medical coverage was excellent, but they weren't about to pay for the schools and accommodations Mina would need. And Bruce insisted they were draining me in other ways, though he didn't know the half of it. I had to leave before I was empty—a husk, a shell, a rind, a robot—he'd come up with a dozen ways to say it. His parents thought we had a case. So we filed and the company settled and then Pop died and I was unemployed and Bruce insisted—depressed—so we left Philly which felt preferable to therapy. We came to Letort, a place I'd never wanted to see again, where nothing had ever been good.

And shockingly, nothing was.

Still, we'd made the effort. We fixed up house and barn, honest physical labor meant to restore a soul. Mine. I even thought it might work. I knew how to put my head down, to plow through and under, but it didn't matter. I'd been joyless for too long, now I was jobless. Useless.

That's when I found the nest.

I should've known he wouldn't believe I'd built a monster. Bruce has never believed in my immense capacity for failure. To create a disaster of this proportion, Solo-sized . . . well, such a thing would take an artist. A mother. And we both know I wasn't either of those, not really. It had to be Big Pharma—because god knows it couldn't have been his wife.

> Do I seem crazy to you, Bruce? Like I've lost my grip?
>
> *That's not what I said.*
>
> Do you?
>
> *I think you need to be with people. Maybe talk to someone. There's no closure here, I was wrong. I'm sorry we ever came. I am so sorry.*

And then my husband, and he is still my husband, put his head down on the table and began to cry. So I told him to get the hell out.

Chapter Eight

A FASTENING OF CROWS

∨

Bruce left, but Ruth was still here. She was everywhere in the goddamned house. And still I kept looking for her.

DAUGHTERS,

What I felt for Eliza confused me.

Her diaries, filled with copies of letters she wrote to others, talk often about her work with indigo, that temperamental crop, as well as her life with her husband, an older man, a widower she loved deeply. Eventually I visited her grave. She died of cancer during a visit to Philadelphia in 1793, the same year yellow fever tore through the city and free blacks, parishioners wrongly assumed to be immune, were enlisted through their churches to nurse the dying and bury the dead and thus, join the dead.

I have tried to counterfeit Eliza's JOY while avoiding this other part of her, how she woke each morning thinking she was devoting herself to both a god and a color that do not exist. And all the while she was ignoring the darkness that moved around and inside her like a parasite.

Nevertheless, I found her voice kind and her desire to be something rather than nothing—comforting. It was not common then for a wife to be matched to a match, so I admired her for a roll of the die, which is not a thing to admire. I also marveled at her intellect. Even if her literacy itself was simply a type of social LUCK *combined with money (*LUCRE*) and* LACK*—there being no adequate son upon whom her father could rely.*

Eliza had her younger sister Polly teach children on the plantation how to read. I suppose she had no time to play governess, not when there were other, lesser women to do it. None of this is admirable, I do know that. You do not keep children under LOCK *and key, not black or girl children, not to learn them their letters or their place, in basement or bedroom, you do not beat them for minor infractions or for their non-belief or because you drank, you do not tell them they are worthless because of what they haven't got between their legs, or that the nothing they carry there is their only source of worth, so often and convincingly there's no coming up from under. No.*

And you do not remain mute as such things are said or done, to a sister, even to the slut of a sister I was, or to yourself, or to your daughters. You do not shut away a girl from the world.

Except of course you have done, you will do, I have done, exactly that. To both of you. How is it possible that I have done that?

My feelings for Ruth have never not presented a difficulty for me.

∨

DEC19

I worked all day building a bal-chatri trap in the barn. The Ladder and Larsen cages on the internet looked too complicated, so I chose one designed for raptors. The trap itself resembles a low tent or a large umbrella made of chicken wire, with nylon monofilament loops strung over it. Pop's fishing line. Next, a lure: my faux sapphire. I don't have a dead turkey on hand, but I don't think Solo will ignore the ring. He has a thing for facets.

I'm about to set the trap out in the pen. When he comes to investigate, his leg will get caught. He's strong enough to lift the mechanism, so I'll need to secure it to the posts. I may even have to tranq him, if he struggles. I bought a dart gun off the internet months ago, just in case, for his mother. American flags all over the website—next to text unironically bragging the weapons' development and production in Germany.

I've been thinking . . . it may be better if Solo did kill the girl. He'd have done it quick, so she wouldn't have suffered. Better that than her bleeding out in some deer blind or brick shack, dragged there for sport by some fuckwit trapper-rapist. Because that's the more common, more likely, more human option.

Bruce left late last night. Mina will be glad to have him back. I shouldn't have called him, it was wrong of me—asking for help. It never turns out well.

∨

POLAROID: *A plate of egg noodles, sunken into a quilt with a leafy free-motion stitch pattern. All threads green, the fabric—a Prussian blue imprinted with ghosts of fern fronds, their curled ends touched with a tea-colored brown.*

R by this point is skeletal, A and B cooking what soft foods they know how to each day. Scrambled eggs and pancakes. Quick breads soaked in cream. She rarely swallows anything but liquid. R does not complain but she grimaces and shudders. Noodles are the favorite, and if they overcook them enough, she can sometimes manage a few spoonsful. If one of them holds the spoon.

A leans over to feed R while B sits on the edge of the bed, gently stroking her legs to distract her from the pain and reduce the swelling, ready to run for the vomit pan, the rags. R wears a diaper now. When they were down at the stove earlier, Pop had come in from inspecting the cover crops for winter rats. He stood for a minute, watching A stir and B fuss with the tray. *Oatmeal's faster*, he said, bending to take off his boots. *Less mess too.*

Harvest was long over, but he'd been leaving them with R all day every day since he'd pulled them out of school. From the upstairs window, they caught glimpses of him stalking the fields with a whittled stick.

When he went to shower, B wiped up the wet grass he'd trailed in. The man still slept in the room with their mother—they assumed he slept—on the hard rocker with a footstool, a flannel blanket behind his head. Often A lay awake, listening to him reading to R from across the hall. She couldn't make out words, but the rhythms sounded to her like poetry. This shocked her and will never be confirmed.

R tries a bite of noodles, spits it out. She looks to A apologetically. *Good*—her eyes glowing—*girl.*

R mimes for B to take a picture of the dish, her voice a rasp. R asks them to document many small things: early sunsets out her window, the crowtree empty at dawn, each other. They cook in part to counteract the smells of her dying—the pictures function in much the same way. Distraction, misdirection, beauty. B badgers her sister for the next two days. Finally, A takes B to the corner of the greenhouse where the unslaked lime is stored. She shows B how she puts it in the milkglass flour shaker to add just a bit to what they cook for R: noodles without onions, bread with no nuts. This would help it be over, and R wants that. It doesn't hurt her, A tells B, firmly.

Once solids are pretty much over, A has B start adding the powder to R's lukewarm tea before climbing the stairs to bend the straw to her cracked lips.

What she said might not be completely right. R has been vomiting less foul brown liquid but more blood. Her sores smell worse. Her eyes have changed—they're never not red now, never not swollen. It is possible, A concedes, that the crows lied to her.

But it is very nearly over, and A wants that. That much is truth.

⌄

T: Agnes, it's Tim.

A: Tim—what time is it?

T: You need to get over here.

⌄

DEC21

I drove to Bethany's. This was two days ago. I haven't been able to write since. I need to go back and put it all down. Keep track. I've had an accident, and it scared me. It's all beginning to scare me.

But first was Scylla.

Solo left the body on the gate. Honor found her when she went out to get eggs—the eggs are Honor's job. She ran back into the house, I guess in a state. Tim was already up. When she'd calmed down enough to tell him what she'd seen, he went to investigate. But he didn't wake Bethany. He called me.

The girl was folded over the fence. Naked. Like a ragdoll Honor said without rags. Tim had wanted to get her down, to cover her, wrap her up, take her out of the cold—a father, making as if the bad-thing-that-happened hadn't. By the time he got the small body into a blanket on the ground, he'd thought better of bringing her inside.

When I got there, she was out beside the pump, swaddled in an old quilt, a Ruth quilt. I knelt in the snow. I opened the rust-and-marigold shroud and folded it back. I examined the cavity where her organs should have been.

Her skin was gauze-colored, the bluish white of a cratered moon. The crater, though, was other colors.

I know how Solo cleans the carcasses I bring to him, and the occasional cat or rabbit I give to him living. I know the pull and snap, the ends of tissues that mark his work, and how he starts with the organs: stomach, liver, kidneys. There was no doubt this . . . breach . . . was his work.

He'd clearly killed this girl, cached her body, and then—instead of taking her down to bone—he'd brought the hollowed child to Bethany. But why? What kind of message was this?

Tim was standing above me. He asked what would make a bird display its kill this way. I asked him why he hadn't woken Bethany.

> *Because *you're* gonna take it away.*

He wasn't going to tell Bethany about the body. I reminded him—Honor had already seen the girl.

> *I'll deal with my daughter. My wife's a wreck . . . Pastor Derek says you're a bad influence.*

That was enough. I walked straight through the house back to her bedroom.

v

Bethany doesn't use store-bought numbing agents: not aspirin, not alcohol. She prefers witch hazel and willow bark but won't hear me out on the potent flavonoids that make them work. Nobody listens to scientists, not here. When he wants a nip, her husband heads to the Tawny. She drinks tea. But Tim let it slip that someone at church had given him some off-brand Ambien so she could rid herself of crow-shaped nightmares and get back to being a mother. Last night he'd finally convinced her to take some.

I shook her. She squinted up at me, groggy.

Ag-nes?

I need you to leave. Take the kids and go.

What are you talking about?

You need to get out of here. Until I can catch Solo.

She pushed to sit up in the bed. I handed her a pillow.

I, we—we're not going anywhere.

Bethany, that girl from the news . . .

I was worried for them but also confused. Birds get hungry, not homicidal. There had to be another explanation for both the killing and his delivery of the body. Some perceived threat? From a child? It didn't make sense. But reasons were irrelevant—this was the second time he'd come to Bethany's. Scylla's body was no shiny token.

Don't watch the news.

Tim said you prayed for her at church.

Wait . . . the Durfee child?

Scylla—yes.

The one whose parents bought the Foultz farm? That girl with no clothes?

I paused, but there was no getting around it.

It was Solo. She's dead.

Bethany looked blankly at me. Tugged up the shoulder of her nightgown.

She was six, they said . . . Merit's seven.

Is she?

I don't know ages. She shook her head, but not at me, she was figuring.

There's nowhere. Tim's dad doesn't have space—since the stroke he's in a trailer. We wanted to bring him here but . . .

I'll give you money. You'll go to a motel.

I laid it out. Scylla was here, Solo had brought the girl to her house, Tim was outside, yes with her, even in this cold, because she's dead, we've got to decide what to do with the body, not just that—no matter what you should go, I mean it, get the kids away from here.

I thought she'd ask about the police. But my sister's sect does not have a good relationship with the law, or the government. Hell, they want out of public school, taxes . . . maybe thinking. I braced myself, waiting for her to resist.

Bury her.

She said it again.

Bury her out by Ruth. Maybe they'll shush then. All fall, they've been grexing—out along the roads gossiping and grexing. They need to shush.

Then the door pushed open. Honor was standing there, twisting the edge of her pajama shirt. Upset. She'd found the body. The girl is only Mina's age—so easy to forget that the way she sister-mothers Forbes. Bethany's birth hadn't turned on any maternal instincts in me. Maybe the two years between us wasn't a big enough gap, or maybe humans were moving beyond the shared parenting of our ape ancestry. Alternately, I suppose I could be missing something. Some necessary hormone.

Bethany made a coaxing gesture with her hand, an insistent reeling of the wrist.

What is it? C'mon, out with it.

Instead of speaking, Honor turned. Merit was standing in the shadows behind her. She put her hand on the little one's shoulder and pushed her into the room.

Bethany immediately sat up straighter, and her face softened. She patted the quilt in front of her encouragingly, a peach-and-turquoise star block. Hers probably—too cheerful to be one of Ruth's. Merit climbed up onto the bed while Honor set up her sister's story: she'd woken to the two of us arguing through the wall, we'd scared her, she had a secret she needed to tell.

Honor nodded at her, *Go on, tell'm what you did me.* Merit looked up at her mother.

The big crow. It came to see me. She added—*A couple times.*

She had a small green bag with her, cinched with a drawstring looped around her wrist. She took it off, opened it, and fished out the proof. There were a handful of items: ripped bit of Mylar, plastic keychain, pickle-jar lid, seashell, industrial screw. She lined them up on the quilt, each on a separate diamond. After they were arrayed, she glanced up at me shyly. Her features are sharper than her mother's, but her eyes are similarly wide set. Open. I smiled back at her.

And where did he leave these? I asked.

By the root cellar where I put the grannies.

Bethany explained that she was in charge of gathering fallen apples from their few dozen trees for the cider press. That was her job. Merit looked proud.

I was scared but Momma says fear of ought-but-God is excuse. So I petted it. It bent down for me. After, if I wasn't there it left things on the bricks.

He'd gotten close enough for her to touch.

Why didn't you tell anyone?

He's just . . . making sure.

Making sure of what?

A whisper: *I'm okay.*

I must've looked unhappy. Merit swallowed hard and glanced down at her treasures. Bethany glared at me before tucking a tangle of bedhead behind her daughter's ear. It took the girl a few seconds, but then she stuck out her chin and defended herself. I like this one.

Honor has Forbes. The boys play soccer and shoot. Serenity can't do things yet. I wanted my own crow.

Bethany nodded sympathetically at her child and pulled her in for a hug. The items on the bed shifted, the screw rolling into the seashell. My sister lifted her face to look me in the eye, her voice tight. *You need to take care of this.*

Honor was still in the doorway. Her voice wavering as she reassured the room.

God won't let what happened to that girl happen to us. Daddy says there must be reasons she was taken.

What reasons? I asked.

He doesn't know. But Pastor says they aren't from around here, the Durfees.

I've noticed there's nothing that scares my sister's new tribe more than questions. The trick, which my niece has already learned, is to imagine an answer that comforts you and attribute it to the parent you wished you had.

Since so few of us have the parent we wish we had, it is imperative that any good American cult provide a surrogate, one with access to all the answers . . . from god, aliens, stock market. I don't think it much matters which.

V

Tim picked up the wrapped body, though I easily could have, and laid it across the backseat of my car. Bethany was still somewhere in the house, kitchen or bathroom, fixing herself or tea. Out of bed at any rate. Honor was sitting in the front window of the house, Forbes in her lap holding a neon green sippy cup with a pink top.

The colors in Bethany's house are skewed, wren colors of unfinished wood and faded cotton bouncing against cheap, parroty plastics. My sister doesn't notice the discrepancy, never has. Neither her faith nor her ceaseless housekeeping keeps her from accruing junk, from shopping at the Dollar General or Walmart when the kids want things she can't find at her church's monthly swaps.

A lifetime ago on a weekend trip up to Cape Cod, Bruce commented on the dowel and dovetail furniture we saw everywhere.

> *Say what you want about zealots, the Shakers at least had an aesthetic.*

My sister does not.

Tim was livid with me for waking her. And he was clear: no police, not poking around his place. He didn't want the body there for a moment longer than it had to be. I agreed to move it but pressed him to take the family to a motel. There's no shortage of roadside lodges nearby, catering to summer tourists from New York City or Philly or DC come to gape at locals, scarf down funnel cakes, try scrapple. But he was adamant.

> *This is my land.*
>
> That's not the point.
>
> *No one's forcing me off my property.*

I wasn't sure if he was referring now to law enforcement or to Solo. I don't know that he knew.

No one is. This is about your kids. Don't you want them safe?

Canon and Prosper already know how to shoot. Honor too.

What?

You don't have to worry about my family. That's my job.

Nothing I could say. He and Bethany are like rusted spigots, impossible to turn. I'd need a saw.

That's when my sister came out. She strode over, big steps.

I'm taking the truck.

I'd never seen her spring this part of herself on her husband. She was channeling her inner Ort. I know because I have one too. From Pop, we both learned how to draw lines in the sand like sinkholes—no one crosses with success.

She told Tim she'd be following me home in the pickup. No, she had no idea how long she'd be. He knew damn well how to fix his own dinner and mind his own kids.

As I was getting into the car, Merit opened the front door. She'd changed from her pajamas into shorts and an oversized t-shirt, purple with silver glitter. I tried to wave her back into the house. She was letting in the cold, her legs were bare. When I got behind the wheel, I saw in my rearview Bethany heading back to the house to have a talk with her daughter, who I was pretty sure could hold her own better than Tim.

I pulled away and avoided Lampeter on the way home. I drove the backroads, carving over and through more hills and hollows the closer I got to the river.

Tim was right but for all the wrong reasons. The body shouldn't stay at Bethany's, and I couldn't call anyone. How could I begin to explain this? There was no way. It'd have to be the barn until I figured what to do.

I opened the window. Had to. The absence of organs and the cold wherever the body'd been these past days had slowed putrefaction, but only slowed it. I spent the half-hour drive in bitter shiver while I contemplated Scylla Durfee's corpse—fingers aching, jaw clenched against chatter, trying to ignore the smell so like and unlike the potatoes I'd let fester.

I should feel responsible, I know that. That's not what I felt.

Her parents needed to be told, they needed to have her body, that was the right thing. But how to give her back to them without incriminating Solo?

When I turned up the drive I heard him, faintly, ahead—his voice low, a series of grating rattles punctuated by brief, sharp notes. He must've gotten caught in the trap, I thought. This was Solo calling out, Solo in pain. What had I done? I stepped on the gas, kicking up gravel. I'd just pulled through the last stand of trees before the house, river birches and aspens, when I saw him, perched on the metal frame of the greenhouse, an edifice of glass cards about to collapse in on itself.

I lost control of the car.

Black ice, Bethany said.

V

The crow's self is itself
nothing but dark
shining.

~BN

Chapter Eight

MY DAUGHTERS,

You may never forgive me, of this I am acutely aware. If people came to visit, if we saw people, your father was certain he would lose me. Or, worse, lose me you.

Eliza Pinckney was also a woman and, thus, unforgivable. Her JOY*—built upon others' suffering—cannot be my subject, though I have been searching and searching for a viable model, one not ruined by the woman who ached to feel it.*

It is difficult to hate a person who took two centuries circling the sun to get to your door. You find yourself offering a chair, some lemonade.

The color Eliza did not know she was after, but I do, is only rarely witnessed in the sky, and only just before it goes completely dark. It a marriage of deepest LAKE *and* BLACK*est denim and it is somehow luminous. I came closest to it the evening I met your father at Speedwell Forge. I was painting at the edge of the water when he came to shore on a rowboat with his catch and approached me, and I asked him if he could see what I was reaching for in the horizon opposite the sunset. He didn't say anything at first, but I saw him look hard and long in the direction I showed him and then at my painting. Only after I'd given up on him answering did he tell me he could see the color and, despite knowing I had captured it not at all, I believed him.*

He saw what I wanted above all things, there, in my own work, where it was precisely not. Although I have never attained the color, not then nor in all the twilights and midnights since, neither on canvas nor quilt, not in the sky nor between your two faces flickering through dream, I have named it. I call it LUCE.

It is a lie, it is your father's, and it is the closest thing to love I've ever known.

V

I woke up in the house, Bethany perched on the coffee table beside me, my face swollen, my leg like knives. I tried to sit up. My body rejected this idea, and my head. Bethany leaned forward to push me gently back down.

You with me now? Stop rutching around—you're hurt.

I was. I tried to talk but struggled with breath, my chest tight. The house smelled like camphor and lemon and something else I couldn't place. I'd been out she said for nearly a day. Something had gone off in the kitchen—so she'd cleared the fridge, checked the mudroom, mopped, and finally gone under the sink where she'd found foul black sludge clinging to a gasket and slip nut.

My sister gave me her assessment: my left femur was probably fractured, plus a rib or two from the seatbelt, my face was pooled in bruise, there were a few cuts. I couldn't see myself, but half my body was united in throb. Merit was there, in the dining room through the archway, her face glowing in the light of Ort's old computer. This didn't make sense, but I couldn't concentrate to think much beyond my pain.

Am I sedated?

My tinctures are at home. All I had was what Tim gave me, some Z-thing—like a begat—Zipporah or Zapheth . . . Zolpidem. You were scaring Merit. I needed to calm you.

The parts of my body I could move felt impossibly heavy, my jaw especially.

What's she doing here?

*She wouldn't stay behind, thinks we're gonna hurt *her* crow.*

Bethany pursed her lips and stood up. On the coffee table beside where she'd been sitting were bowls and bandages. Damp towels. A pair of scissors.

What the fuck, Bethany.

Hush!

She waved across the room toward Merit.

Why didn't you take me to the hospital?

Then you'd be sick on top of injured. We got you into the house . . . Nothing broken on you that needs more than a splint and a poultice. And there was the girl to think of.

She didn't mean Merit. I stared at the wall in front of me. Off-white, paint over patched plaster prone to flaking. Bruce had sanded and oiled the wood trim, adding what he thought were calming colors to the room, accent pieces in sea foams and slates. A denim rag rug, throw pillows, vases. Oceanic colors on rearranged deck chairs.

I thought, I'm taking on water, and that felt right, to acknowledge things were deteriorating. Me—filling up with the cold dark, each breath sharp. I was back where I'd always been. Why did I think I could ever get to somewhere else?

Where's Solo?

Don't know. I was halfway up the drive when I saw you rolled the car. The roof's a mess but it was back on its wheels and, blessfully, your door opened. The girl was thrown out the back.

Scylla.

Merit stayed with you. I took the body to the greenhouse, put her under a tarp. I thought we might have to call someone, but you came to. Sort of. Leastways we got you inside.

She looked over at Merit, but the child was engrossed. Her face kept changing through spectrums of color from the shifting screen.

The greenhouse, of course. Scylla's body, broken down, might be just the thing to resurrect Ruth's flowers—her hydrangeas and hyacinths, gardenias and chrysanthemums, lilies and tulips. What would I need to add to help the process along?

This was the sleeping pills, and I tried to shake the vision off. I shut my eyes tight, which hurt.

> *I brought Pop's crutches down from the attic. He hated them, called himself a useless cripple . . . but I told him cripples aren't useless. They can do things.*

I cringed at the word . . . as Bruce had taught me to. There were others I was supposed to also avoid but that one stuck—I could now hear its wrongness. I realized, vaguely, that my sister was trying to be kind. About Mina. She pointed to the windowsill. The crutches were propped there. Ort sprained his ankle the summer after Bethany'd had Honor. She, Tim, the boys, and the baby had moved back in with him for a month to help with the harvest. I hadn't known. I hadn't thought about anything that year but keeping my daughter alive.

The sun was ducking in and out of clouds. Bethany said we had work to do. Now I was up, she was going to shower. It took some wrangling, but she got Merit off the computer and sent her over to put *an angel kiss on top of Auntie's head* before taking her upstairs.

They've been up there now for over an hour. I managed to sit up. Ruth's diary is here and my journal. I've been filling in gaps. The last thing I wrote—it was how I'd sent Bruce away.

Too many things slipping out of place. I can't afford to lose anything else.

Chapter Eight

I shuffled my way out onto the porch.

The Krahn house, built on a rise, faces south, giving it a view of fields and the long drive curving to the left, through a copse of trees and some brush—azalea and holly, bayberry and blackthorn—all bramble now. There's fields, then a hollow, then a ridge to the west. The river's not three miles. I hobbled over to the far-right corner to look back beside the house at the locust tree, invisible from the front door. A dozen or so crows were there, silent in the bright midday. High noon is not their happy hour.

The wind must've picked up then because the planks groaned under me. The entire structure, which was not original to the house, needed replaced before we put it on the market—first thing our realtor told us. Bruce and I never let Mina out on the porch, it was too dangerous. In another life, one that doesn't seem real now, we'd talked about doing the work ourselves.

My phone buzzed, Bruce's number, and the birds failed to react. A few already turned in my direction may have blinked, their shrewd eyes flashing like abacus beads.

> *Mom, are you there?*
>
> Mina. I'm here, what is it?
>
> *I . . . I miss you. Dad's worried, I can tell. He keeps asking me to play chess and I don't like playing chess. I get stiff.*

The wind ruffled the crows' feathers. They themselves were immobile, listening.

> So tell him you don't want to. And tell him there's nothing to worry about.
>
> *Can you come for Christmas? Halmoni and Poppy said that'd be fine.*

I don't think so. It's—not possible.

Why not?

Because.

I didn't know what to say. I needed to take care of Solo. My mistakes couldn't find their way to my daughter, not this time. I hate that it was better, but it was. Us, apart.

Something's happened to the car.

Wait, what? *but—(some mumbling)* *We could come get you.*

Did he . . . is your dad there? Did he tell you to call?

(pause)

Mina?

I'm knitting you a scarf. Halmoni and I are learning together—she's already done a blanket. Dad said maybe you could be here to give it to. Mine might not be done . . . I'm getting faster though.

Tell your dad I'll call when I can.

Mom?

Yes?

I love you.

I'll call soon. Promise.

Ort had died on the porch, stepped through a rotten plank up to his thigh. It cut him deep and he'd bled out. The mailman found him intact, except for his eyes—most scavengers go for the eyes first. The mortician told us it could've been worse . . . if he'd died inside, with pets. Told us he'd seen that with older people, a few times, and it wasn't pretty. We didn't have an open casket, Bethany made all the arrangements. Ort had been nearly eighty. I nailed plywood over the hole.

Chapter Eight

The pain in my leg was making me dizzy. That, or falling blood sugar. I lowered myself into Pop's rocker, pushed by wind against the railing.

The boards beneath me were shredded, whole sections of gray paint stripped, revealing the graying pine beneath and, in the gaps—the crawlspace below, easily accessed by pulling back loose latticework beside the six steps that led up to the porch. Fastidious as she was, Bethany took to playing dolls under there after Ruth died, babbling to an imaginary friend, Toby, resurrected from her toddlerhood. She was too old for dolls and I told her so. I told her it was dirty, to be down there, with a boy, even an invisible one. She cried. But I didn't like that any better.

While Ruth was still sick, Pop used to sit on the porch for hours.

Pain made it harder for her to suppress her spiraling speech. She would loop over and over the same subjects with slight permutations, as if with every pass she was getting closer to another reality. A preferable one. Bethany would go around tidying then because when Ruth was like that she stopped keeping house. I'd climb into a book, nearby. Probably L'Engle: *Arm of the Starfish, A Wrinkle in Time, The Moon by Night.* If I wandered too far from where she was nattering, Pop would say, *Go be with your mother. She needs tended to.* Once, but only once, I asked why I couldn't read on the porch and him do the tending. He fixed me with a stare I can't describe, except it was nails. Ring-shanked pole-barn nails. I wasn't going anywhere.

In the past hour, Merit's peeked out a few times to ask some questions about the computer, the house, me. She's helping her mom make eggs. Dippy, my favorite.

I've just been informed, hers too.

V

The year before she died, Miss Deb fell into a diabetic coma. Collapsed at church. Once she woke up, I went to visit her at the hospital. She took one look at me and insisted I'd come there to kill her.

It felt like a slap.

Her jewels, I wanted them, she was convinced. Drawerfuls of painted beads and costume glass, her trove of shiny things. I knew them all, of course. They signified moods she wanted to be in, festive or regal or not-to-be-messed-with. They were a talking-to she gave herself when she wasn't up to the day. They let other people know she had value, was a person *of* value. She threatened to evict me. She called me a bloodsucker, a vulture, a whore. It was harrowing because—fury or no—she looked fragile without her wig. Without her helmet of pewter curls, her eyes were bigger, wilder. Like a child's, or the eyes of the dying. I bolted before her day nurse Jill could explain.

Seems delusions are common in the ICU. Miss Deb remembered not a thing she'd said to me. Later she asked where I'd gone off to—her emergency contact, her friend, that girl scientist—and Jill let her know. She was mortified. She made Jill call me. When I came back the next morning, Miss Deb took my hand in both of hers and told me she'd been out of her right mind. My hands were chapped as always from the lab. Just a few weeks before, Miss Deb had left Palmer's lotion and night gloves for me in a giftbag in the kitchen. I hadn't used them, was ashamed I hadn't. Her own hands were warm and soft and veined from age.

Within days of her release, when she should've been recuperating, she cooked me my favorite casserole: cheddar, yellow squash, and bacon. She normally wore at least six silver rings, among them a large emerald piece, probably glass—which she took off for dishes but not to cook. She was a force. While she was spooning a bowlful out, its green eye flashed up at me. She joked.

I did catch you eyeing my lapis lazuli opera necklace that one time, though.

What I'm saying is I think it might not be real, what I overheard.

I limped around the house to go look where he'd been, to see if Solo'd left any sign near the greenhouse or garden. Nothing. The inner door to the mudroom was open—Ruth had always opened it when she was at the stove. I heard my sister and Merit through the screen door. Or—more likely?—I invented the conversation.

B: What kind of a Krahn doesn't grow parsley on the sill?

M: Which one is parsley?

B: The three-leaf with the frilly edge. The one I use to make the butter.

M: The green butter for cuts.

B: Yes.

M: Should I go look for an oak?

B: There's no good oak close by. Oma made notes.

M: Was it Oma who taught you?

B: No. She was gone before I was born. I only have her books. Pop was the one should've carried it forward, but he didn't believe.

M: Why didn't he?

B: He was a man. Plus he shut his eyes hard against the Lord. Like your aunt Agnes.

M: Can she see Him now?

B: Not see. But God is making it so she can't ignore him . . . *And suddenly there came a sound from heaven as of a rushing wind, and it filled all the house where they were sitting. And there appeared unto them cloven tongues as of fire, and it sat upon each of them.*

M: Is God the fire?

B: The holy ghost chooses different forms. It comes as it will. It does as it will.

Whatever I heard, I went back around to the front, fumbled myself up onto the porch and back into the house. A few minutes later Bethany brought me my eggs. She told me to eat and then get dressed, bundle up. She went to the greenhouse for a shovel and the body. It was time she said for us to go see Ruth.

∨

DEC22

There's too much. It feels impossible to set down with accuracy, but I have to try.

After I wrote some and ate some, we headed out. It was midafternoon, Bethany carrying Scylla's corpse swaddled in the blood-and-mustard quilt, me on crutches with the shovel belted across my back—we might've been a couple of local preppers, heading to our bunker for the end times.

We left Merit at the house. Bethany insisted. She said it was fine, that Honor'd been babysitting a year by this age. Merit had my phone, she was on the computer, we wouldn't be long, two hours at most. My sister doesn't coddle children but, as fourth in line, her daughter couldn't have been alone much.

I hadn't been out there, where we were headed, not since the day we buried Ruth.

Pop had followed his wife's instructions. She wanted her body unboxed and put under a tree. It was still legal in our state to have a home burial, and she made him swear. After the viewing, a nod to the weepy Cullens, brothers and cousins, Pop brought her home. There wasn't much fuss about that, not from the men, anyway.

She didn't want to be buried on Krahn ground. There's a family plot overgrown in the copse that Ruth had always steered us from: eight or nine disintegrated stones. Poison ivy, she said, nettles and nastiness. Pop told us there were far more than that, scattered around, unmarked.

Family lore was at least one child had been buried up by the house so his mother could visit him daily.

An old willow leaned over a sometime-stream less than a mile from the edge of the north field. Technically, this spot was on Sensenig land, a corner they'd left to rewild. We'd gone there for spring picnics when we were young, but only when the stream was flowing. Droughts made Ruth sad—here, and in Africa. The crumbling bank also made her sad, as did wildfires in California. The cracked creek bed, domestic violence, oil spills, dwindling ozone. Islands of plastic in the Pacific. I don't know why she subjected herself to the radio. She said the patterns calmed her, history revisiting itself, a predictable replaying. But I lived with her quilts. Her designs were the opposite of soothing.

She told me once not to make the mistake of loving a thing only partway, only when it loves you back. I thought she was talking about the dry stream. Now I think no. She meant the world, all its contradictions kneaded together, mixed up and blistering her mind—yeasty. Metamorphic.

A week after she died we were trudging through the snow, her body slung over Pop's shoulder in a sack. Until late spring, the stream ran into another, one active enough to have a name, and that crick, Alder's Run, ran into the Conestoga, the Conestoga into the Susquehanna, Susquehanna into Chesapeake, Chesapeake to Atlantic.

Next year, the fallen leaves will take your mother with them. To the ocean.

Because I knew she'd never been, Pop's words, spoken through thick breaths, sounded like tenderness. I was embarrassed for him.

He'd come out the day before to hack through the frozen ground. There would be no marker he told us. Just the tree. He heaved her off his shoulder and let her fall. I winced. Her body sounded like a body dropped a fathom into the ground. He picked up the shovel he'd left at the base of the willow—he'd brought the pick home—covered her over, then tamped down the earth. It took a long time, it was cold, and Bethany and I were by the end shifting from foot to foot. That felt wrong. It all did.

There were no words after. He didn't say any, didn't ask us for ours. We hurried home in the onset of a silence that would last until he died.

Because of the crutches, my ribs, the snow, it took Bethany and me a half-hour to make it to the spot. Everything was the same, except this time there was no grave waiting. Bethany would have to dig it. The earth wasn't frozen yet and she was strong. I don't know why I'd agreed to come back to this place. We'd argued while we trudged through the field. I was slow from my injuries. She was slow because the emptied girl, though empty, was still cumbersome.

We should leave her where the police can find her.

They'd figure out a way to blame us.

Why do you think this would come back on you?

It would. This'll work—it did before.

You're telling me you've buried a child before?

I have. But you're not really asking me that, you're making a joke.

I was, but . . . my sister had lost a child, or a pregnancy—something formed enough to bury—and not told me? It was almost unthinkable that she'd kept such a thing from me. But it was also oddly protective *of* me.

> What are you saying?
>
> *I'm saying it worked with the crows. After Momma died, after we put her in the earth, they stopped asking for things.*

And back to her superstitious drivel.

> You're serious.
>
> *Don't pretend. Stop pretending it was a dream. It wasn't. She heard them, we did. They want what they want.*
>
> And what is that?

She turned to me. At that moment, Scylla in her arms was Mina in Bruce's. That's what I saw. How long will it be until he can't carry her anymore—until she won't let him?

Bethany looked down at the swaddling.

> *I don't know why this girl needed to die. I do know God wanted to take Momma, and she and Pop flat out refused Him. For years. The crows are His dark mirrors.*
>
> You're scaring me.

Her face shot up, eyes narrow.

> *You think you're smarter than God, but that twists everything around. He wanted Ruth. Her fighting Him—that's what opened us up to the shadows.*
>
> Oh Bethany, you have indeed been opened.

It was worse than I'd thought. She wasn't simply in a cult. Bethany was smart enough to use what she'd heard from those Pentecostal pieces of shit to bend the world, to translate our entire lives through the lens of the supernatural. That's how the fucking things work.

God had nothing to do with this. I was out in the snow, ready to bury a little girl's body *because* I knew there was no god. Because Scylla Durfee was dead and I could do nothing to reverse it and because, if I was honest, I did not know this child. Later, I could send an anonymous letter. Tell her parents she was dead. I could give her abstract family abstract closure. This rotting body would give no one comfort, and none of that had to happen now—I could do the right thing once I had found and recaptured Solo. That was how this had to go. That was the order of operations.

I felt bad, I did. But it was logic dictating my actions, not goddamned magical thinking.

Bethany placed the body on the ground and took the shovel from my back. The digging would take some time and I was in no shape to help. I drifted over to where I thought Ruth should be. The earth was slightly sunken there. I shambled around the shallow trough, ducking through branches. My feet were getting numb and my thigh had begun to throb. Not good—we still had the hike back.

Long before our mother's death, Bethany and I named the nameless creek Mousetail. It bent if you followed it, and when it dried up each summer we joked the farmer's wife had gotten it. It wasn't a good picture, not the right picture to have in my mind, a wild Ruth running round the willow with a butcher's knife. I looked down to the water.

It was warmer than it had been all morning, some melt, water moving like a snake through a gulley. I whispered.

Momma?

She didn't answer. I hadn't expected to feel anything and I didn't. Bethany stopped digging and looked over. She'd known the child

I'd been when she was even younger. Those girls were long gone, buried here too.

Bethany gasped then.

She dropped the shovel and pointed to the other side of the stream. To Solo.

The bird stood obsidian against the snow—bright black in winter light. He took two steps toward us then bowed his head almost to his feet. I always thought he looked like a knight on a chessboard when he did that, the curve of his spine gracious. Equine. He bent his legs then, and lengthened himself, lowering his entire body to the snow-covered ground. A few seconds poised like an arrow, and he drew himself back up to his full height. It was a strange dance. Had he grown since he'd left? Looked like he might've.

Agnes, let's go.

Bethany whispered beside me, her hand on my upper arm. I leaned hard onto one crutch to reach out to the bird. The other fell into the snow. Solo startled, hopping twice, a quarter turn away and back. Something wasn't right. Bethany's grip tightened. She was clutching me, holding me and her breath both. My sister could talk a brave game, but Solo's presence unmoored her.

The distance between us and the bird was less than fifteen feet over the stream. A wingspan.

Solo? I said.

He didn't answer.

Solo. I scolded him.

He hopped again, his wings fluttering out, then settling. He tilted his head, blinked. I waited.

Bad bring.

Thank god. He still knew me.

Yes, I agreed. Yes, very bad.

And then Solo shook his head—a child correcting a willfully obtuse adult.

Agnes. Agnes bad bring.

Nothing, of course, could have been truer.

But before I could respond, before I could apologize for selfishly drawing him out of his shell and into a world that would hate him, for depriving him of his real mother, for keeping him locked away for reasons he couldn't grasp if I offered them, reasons I'm not sure were valid, or even true—he spread his immense wings and pushed into the sky.

Bethany released my elbow. And I saw, in the snow where the bird's feet had been, blood.

My sister's scream pierced the gray.

Oh my God—Merit—

We left Scylla under the willow. Bethany sprinted across mud and snow through the woods over the long hill to the north field and back up to the house. I followed as fast as I could on the crutches, half-hopping, half-limping. I fell twice, but picked myself up and went after my little sister.

I did not believe the blood was Merit's.

Bethany would say this is because I do not know how to believe.

Chapter Nine

A HAZARD OF CROWS

This next part is harder.

I need to be methodical. I need not to embellish or swerve from observation into speculation. Analysis comes later, interpretation. Conclusion. Right now I need to record what happened. I will try to keep myself to that.

When I got back to the property, I didn't head to the house. I knew Bethany would be there. If Merit was missing, it would save time if I were looking elsewhere. Divide-and-conquer was my thinking. I staggered into the pen.

I could barely make it out, the trap I'd set. It was chaos, a snarl of metal twisting against itself like some modern art nightmare. Calder, unstrung—was it Calder? Bruce would know.

I moved closer on my crutches. It hurt to breathe and my underarms were raw from the trek back. I put some weight on the left leg with each step. Every time I did this, a shot of pain coursed from knee to hip. More damage maybe, from one of my falls. Bethany's backwoods splint could only do so much—bandages smashing my thigh between halves of an old cutting board she'd split in two.

Mina has negotiated metal-and-plastic contraptions since she was a toddler, without complaint. Does that mean she didn't have pain? Or that she's always had it? Maybe it means she has a more honest relationship with her body, that she pays attention to how it works, what it feels. There are parts of me so long neglected I wouldn't know where to start.

Once I got inside the pen, I examined the twisted concavity, tossed upside down but still attached to a fence post. Much of the fishing line I'd knotted was hanging loose, severed from its loops. I didn't understand how. That should require a more precise instrument than Solo's beak. He hadn't been pleased to find it here, but it clearly posed no problem for him. My ring was nowhere to be found. I drug the end of one crutch through the mud, searching for a glint. What had I been thinking? Yet another part of myself I'd willingly sacrificed to this enormous crow.

Miss Deb would've been furious. That ring was her kind of gesture, its message one she'd repeated often—everyone deserves love. Yes. Even me. Clearly she had no idea who she'd invited into her home.

I looked up and saw a different memo.

There, on the side of the barn facing the pen, Solo had gouged two huge crescents into the weathered, painted wood. One above, one below, facing different directions. They touched where they met in a jagged S.

Merit!? Merit, where are you? Answer me, Merit!

Bethany was up at the house, yelling from porch or side door. I couldn't see her. The day had entered the half-dark of late afternoon, weighty clouds moving in. I heard her through the wind, which was picking up. I wanted to call back to her, but I was afraid she would think I'd found Merit.

Chapter Nine

And I was afraid I would find Merit.

I went toward the peeling place without my sister. As I made my way over to the barn, I spoke to the universe. Please, please don't let her be in here.

The universe laughed at me. Praying.

⌄

It was dim inside. Damp hay assaulted my nostrils. The wind moaned. I hadn't been inside the barn in days. When my eyes adjusted, I saw something was wrong—violently off.

The wall where Solo made his marks was shredded. I limped towards it. The work had been decimated, pieces of wood ripped from the most densely scrawled-on areas. I felt slapped. Was this Solo telling me he no longer wanted to communicate? Did he think me a thief—that I'd steal his art? Was this him renouncing this place, this prison, and me as jailer?

A flash on the ground drew my eye from the wall. Glass.

Once I saw it, I saw it was everywhere. I looked up. The wind was keening, but not outside, up in the rafters. The western skylight was gone—all but two jagged triangles clinging to the bottom of the frame, leaning in. And above and between them, charcoal cloud.

A few seconds later, in flew a standard crow. The bird shot through the gap like a shadow, slalomed through the roof beams, then headed lower. It zipped past me as if I weren't there and sunk its talons into the ragged wall. Somehow it balanced like that, like a woodpecker, though it shouldn't be able, as crows have anisodactyl, not zygodactyl feet . . . a puzzle for another time.

The bird started picking at an exposed splinter, then spat it to the ground. It ripped out two more, three. The last one was larger.

This was the one. Once it wrested it from the shiplapped boards, the crow hopped down onto the barn floor and drug the wood a few times through the hay, clearing a small space before dropping the sliver in the center.

Then it took off, up to the rafters and out.

I looked at the floor below the ratty wall and saw several such clearings. Altars—and at the center of each—a relic. A wooden sliver, a shard of glass, a lock of bloody hair.

Merit whimpered then.

V

I was able to coax her out of the corner of the stall where she was huddled, cold and shook. Her hair was a wet red nest, her face ravaged, the front of her shirt stiff and sticking to her, its glitter dark. Once out, she wouldn't let go of my good leg. There was no way we could reach the house with her clinging like that. At the door of the barn, I yelled for Bethany. The child wasn't speaking, at least not to me.

Bethany came sprinting down the hill from the house. This had been our sledding hill, from house to barn, the slope steep. I thought she was going to barrel through us, but when she got just a few yards away, she pulled herself up short.

Dear Lord in Heaven.

I thought we must look worse than I imagined, but that was not where her eyes were. I turned to my right, following her gaze toward pen and pond. I couldn't see anything. So I dragged Merit out to where my sister was. Bethany came a few steps closer, grabbed her daughter, and hugged her tight. Merit's arms went limp. My sister crouched down and took Merit's face between her hands to get a good look at her. But also she would not let her turn.

Just past the corner of the structure, on the ground beneath Solo's S, I saw a mound of crimson and gold that wasn't there when I'd entered the barn.

I made my way closer. Below Solo's signature lay Ruth's quilt in a wet heap. But that couldn't be right—it was back at the willow, with Scylla. I squinted harder. I saw it then, the small gray hand. It extended, palm up, just beyond the edge of the fabric. It was darkened and shriveled. Tiny. And then I registered what at first I hadn't made out within the folds of quilt: the slight contours of a body.

She was here. He'd brought her back.

I heard something then. A gust. Wind, and a tapping from above. After a moment, there was another rush of air. On the gutter up above my head, ten crows had landed.

Seconds later—a dozen more joined them. Each new arrival strained the metal further. It groaned. Soon there were a hundred jockeying for position on the roof.

Then two hundred.

I looked to Bethany. Merit was breathing quickly and burrowing into her mother. She was turned away from me, but I could see her whole body cringing at the sound of the birds. I waved at my sister to go. She didn't hesitate. She scooped up her daughter and started walking as quickly as she could up the hill. The light was on in the kitchen. I could see Merit's eyes over her mother's shoulder, frightened moons.

The waves kept coming onto the barn until bird and bird-shadow darkened the tin slope above me. Some slipped down the snow-wet metal to replace others at the bottom who, disgruntled, settled elsewhere.

I should've left then.

Their deliberations started low. There was some tittering, a few caws, before those sounds were drowned out by others, vocalizations so agitated they lifted the birds off the roof for a few manic seconds before they dropped down again to reassert their dominance. Tapping, shuffling sounds of feet and wings against tin, against each other, underscored murmurings that made chatter at first, then argument. Rusty caws dragged their nasal sound against buzzier rattling. They were fighting with each other. I saw one bird peck another's chest. A large one closed his beak over the beak of the smaller crow beside him. For a few moments, they wrested heads like serpents. All over the roof, skirmishes erupted. I'd never seen the crows act this way. Never. Not in the locust tree or in Pop's fields, not even fighting over the peanuts Bethany liked to throw at them across the snow when we were young, when Ruth insisted we were to keep them contented, especially in winter, in times of scarcity.

I instinctively backed up. This was difficult on crutches, and I stumbled but somehow kept from going down. They were dropping off the roof now, a few at a time, nearly hitting the ground before regaining flight. Two, squalling in midair, unable to reverse their fall, landed on their backs.

On the quilt.

They must've caught her scent then because suddenly they unlocked talons and, in a frenzy of a different key, started pulling at the fabric, tugging it between them until beneath their fray the corpse was uncovered. I saw her body, in that moment, in a way I hadn't. At Bethany's I'd been weighing evidence, gruesome proof of Solo's nature. Now I saw something else.

Scylla's dusky fawn-like limbs were bent at wrong angles. A half-braided knot of matted hair hung over her mottled face. Here was a darkened sliver of the light Scylla must've been in life. A fingernail clipped from the world. Someone's child.

I caught this glimpse before they descended, spilling over the edge of the roof in black avalanche.

The pulse and sweep of their wings kept other sounds from reaching me. An arrhythmic tide. Had she been alive, the girl would've been screaming, but the only shrieks were birds'. There was no gurgle of living throat, rent. No wet snap of calf muscle or pectoral flayed from bone by beak. Not even the dry rip of desiccated jerky. And though it was happening just there, a few yards in front me, I did not hear the crack and pop of vertebrae wrested apart by crows at different ends of spine, her child-body like hard taffy.

I heard wind. It sounded like fire. I saw a writhing hill of wings. Among them, I saw heads yanked back with the effort incurred by a stubborn tendon. Or maybe these beaks, raised into sky, were gestures to the hunter Orion—meant to express gratitude for his kill.

But no. This was Solo's doing.

I do not know what they were saying. I do not want to know.

⌄

I backed away slowly.

After what felt like an hour, I turned and crept toward the house so as not to draw attention.

My faltering gait, the uneven rhythm of crutch and foot, my labored breaths—all these marked me as prey. Soft target.

⌄

Merit was cleaned and bandaged by the time I reached the house and got myself up the stairs.

Bethany and I sat on the bed on either side of her, on Ruth's deathbed—at least on its pine frame. Pop burned the mattress when he relocated himself to the attic. He'd taken away the piles of books strewn all over the house, the swatches she tacked to the walls to test their colors in different light. He removed her from anywhere she was. I thought he was trying to erase her, but now I think this was his version of hoarding. Tidy and mean.

Merit had told Bethany it wasn't Solo who'd hurt her. It was the others.

After we'd left for the willow, she went out onto the front porch to wait for the snow. Bethany says her daughter smells it coming. Merit was sitting on the stairs when they attacked.

They'd gone for her head—ripping her hair out by the roots and leaving more than a dozen jagged cuts on her scalp, neck, and face. I thought my sister had brought up tea for the child, but she dipped a washcloth into the mug on the bedside table and dabbed it onto Merit's wounds.

> What's that?
>
> *Boiled birch water. Bark from the first tree along the drive.*
>
> Bethany . . .
>
> *It works. It's natural. It'll prevent scarring—more importantly, it'll protect her.*

Bethany wasn't saying much, but I could see she was beside herself with thoughts of evil. I wanted to tell her this was no demon, no devil, no dark mirror. This was birds.

The dive-bombing Merit described is not unknown in crows. It happens soon after fledglings leave their nests. The parents of the adolescent birds become hypervigilant, attacking strange or unpredictable humans, whom they view as threats to their vulnerable progeny. Merit, at seven years old, is about as unpredictable as our species comes.

If they'd been trying to kill her, I've no doubt they would have.

Don't mistake me—I was frightened—something had gone haywire in them. It's rational to be scared on a cliffside, in the ocean, around wild animals, and I'd just witnessed a feeding frenzy. I too was disturbed. I had no idea what was compelling their behavior, but it wasn't the Antichrist. And I've no understanding of how such ideas comfort Bethany, just that they seem to.

What confused me most was the crows' sense of kinship to Solo. It was the explanation of their attack on Merit that made the most sense. Did this roost somehow view him as their collective offspring? These weren't crows I'd bred. These weren't crows he knew.

How did you get away? I asked Merit.

Bethany shook her head in frustration. She'd obviously also asked this question.

Mine came then. He came and he picked me up and hid me. He didn't mean to . . .

Then my niece lifted up the faded dandelion of an old concert tee my sister had found among my things—The Innocence Mission. Blood was seeping through a massive bandage on her torso in a diagonal slice from nipple to appendix. Bethany yanked down the shirt.

That's enough now. You need sleep.

The girl is seven. But skin is still a thing for Bethany. Shame.

By Ruth's end, two of her largest tumors were stretching out her abdomen like warring fetuses. During too-brief respites from her pain, she'd lift her shirt to trace the lumps with skeletal fingers in half-gloves. She was always cold. Mortified, Bethany would try to cover her back up. Ruth said they waxed and waned against each other, her moons . . . her abdo-moon-als. And she'd laugh. Her laugh glimmered, quaking aspen leaves, bright as yellow. My sister and I for three years tended this vanishing thing that kept hinting backwards to a woman who'd never been there, not fully.

Out the window I could see the locust. It was, for the time being, empty.

And Ruth's ghost? She was not in this house. Not anymore.

⌄

They will refuse to
bleed. Shoot a crow
and seeds like rubies

spill. Sow these—
and need roots. Ill
omen, iller weed.

~BN

⌄

We came downstairs, and Bethany headed into the kitchen. The adrenalin was wearing off and my leg and ribs were aching. I dropped bone-tired onto the couch, shut my eyes, fell into dream.

The fields were on fire. The sky was smoke and beyond that—stars—a realm of unreachable calm. Mina was leading me to the river. In the distance, Bethany stood waist-deep in rushing water, washing out a bloody dress, the way to her blocked. A current of red ran downstream from her hands, rubbing and rubbing together the cloth.

Mina was close to the ground where there was less smoke. *Crawl*, she whispered. *Crawl.*

Chapter Nine

I heard a shot. A tree snapped above us, a huge bough. I threw myself forward, covering her body with my own.

Another shot.

I woke then. I was on the couch under a heavy quilt I'd brought down in November for days I didn't make it up the stairs—a motley of gray-blacks, umbers, and sepia, dark-to-light in a radiating pattern, like something burnt. Bethany must've thrown it over me.

Bethany?

She didn't answer. I got up and limped to the front door, each half-step an electric jolt. I reached the porch to find my sister aiming Ort's rifle back beside the kitchen, at the locust. I spoke calmly.

Where'd you get that?

The greenhouse. They won't move.

What do you mean?

They started coming in fifteen minutes ago, from all directions. I yelled. Nothing. I ran toward them but they're like stone, so I got the gun. That's twice I shot.

Pointless though the gesture was, it impressed me. I'd forgotten how fierce my sister could be. She held her stance.

You hit one?

I'm saying they didn't move.

They didn't scatter, at all?

No.

The whole time she spoke, the gun was braced against her shoulder. I made my way to her, touched her elbow, bringing her arm down and, with it, the rifle. I looked over to where she'd been aiming. It wasn't clear at first, what I was looking at.

The sun's corona was orange behind cirrus clouds, the sky puce and darkening. Beyond the locust, the white field sloped away from the house, broken yellow stalks like the segmented legs of massive dead insects upturned in snow. The tree itself looked thick . . . no. Teeming. The branches were so dense with birds the limbs should've given way. Normally, crows perch only in the outer and uppermost branches, but these numbers were ten times any gathering I'd seen.

They thronged shoulder to shoulder on every available foothold. Others balanced on the six-inch spikes that jutted out in star-forms from the bark. It looked less like a roost than an infestation, wings glistening like beetle shells, light from the kitchen window rippling across the tree in alien shimmer.

They weren't moving. Not turning their heads, not preening, not shifting from foot to scaly foot. Neck feathers ruffled by cold wind was all. The tree was a single organism, a quiver of life, frozen. Insects are expert at such stillness. But vertebrates can also achieve this uncanny quiet—when they are being hunted.

Or when they're being hunters.

Bethany, let's go inside.

v

We didn't know what to do with ourselves. I suggested we wake Merit and leave. Bethany told me not to be stupid, it was late, heavy snow on its way. We'd head to her place come morning.

You want to call Tim?

What would Tim do?

Bethany headed to the kitchen.

Chapter Nine

˅

DAUGHTERS,

I did not choose willingly to return.

My parents sent me to school against their best judgment, but they didn't want me back, damaged as I was. Patrick and Ian had already moved on from Coral Street, and Charlie and Hen were nearly out of our small brick house. I'd left the church when I was twelve, and the priest advised my parents against revisiting my influence on my younger brothers.

So I was sent to live with my great-aunt Lissa across town to help her with her quilts. She was hard of hearing, didn't mind me talking out loud while we worked so long as I stitched my knots close. She gave me a space to set up my easels, a front room where passersby could gawk at my unreasonable growth. I liked to take my canvases around to the river and hills, and lakes, en plein air, like any good impressionist. Lissa had her dead husband Tuck's '72 Ford Bronco half-cab she let me drive, and I hauled my easel and paint box all over the county.

Outside I could keep the fumes I inhaled to a minimum. Cadmium and cobalt are toxic, but fresh air would counteract any damaging effects on the fetus. And I did worry. My mother adored Jerry Lewis and his telethon, and we used to hunker down in front of our twelve-inch with popcorn every Labor Day. Every year she'd tell my dad to call in and pledge, and every year he told her we had enough defects to worry about in our own damn house. My mother's softer word for me was touched.

I was six months along when I met Ort out by the water. He had sad brown eyes and I found him there often. He'd be on the lake fishing when I was setting up, but after an hour or so he'd come by even if he hadn't caught anything to look at my work. He asked no questions, but I answered anyway, drawing the connections between—

LIGHT/GUILT *VALUE/VIOLENCE*

COLOR/CRUELTY *SHAPE/SHAME*

> *I knew this man wouldn't hurt me. I could tell those battles were done in him.*

Pain made it hard for me to keep reading Ruth. It's possible I was feverish—I'd overdone by any measure. I put a pillow under my leg and held the ice Bethany'd brought in a towel above my kneecap. I'd asked her for a whiskey, which she handed me, frowning, before heading back to the kitchen. I heard water running, a broom. I took a few good burning sips before reading on.

∨

Ruth had been pregnant when she'd met Ort. In spite of everything going on around me, this bit of history was news. News I needed to understand.

> *After a few weeks, I asked Ort if we should get married which he said made good sense, if I didn't mind his age. I laughed. The religion professor who'd taken me under his wing and into his private rooms was much older, sixty-four to your father's forty-six. That wasn't why I was kicked out, not exactly. I'm guessing Dr. Savadze claimed a crazy girl threw herself into his bed. I didn't throw myself, my daughters, trust me that the bed was far too high. I may indeed be crazy, but crazy is not my suchness.*

> *That whole spring, I'd been training into the city on the weekends to sketch by Eliza Pinckney's grave and argue with her about education and womanhood. Eventually logic dictated that I must be the who/m I was arguing with, perhaps Eliza reincarnate, though I don't remember my exact theory. I do know that one May evening, despondent after my final crit, I hoed up a small patch of land behind the dining hall, and the next day began recruiting workers I planned to educate holistically. To my credit, my idea was to pay them well, but the local elementary school principal*

brought me in from the playground to his office and called my dean who, in turn, called my parents. Dean Halsey told them I needed serious psychiatric help and gently, foolishly, suggested an abortion might be the prudent thing.

Aunt Lissa was what I got. She didn't mind me calling myself Eliza for a few weeks, until Mrs. Pinckney played herself out of me. I'd guess hormones had worsened my unfortunate chemistry, but I'm no doctor, and won't see one. On this your father and I are agreed. The shrinks at the VA drugged him into stupor for a decade, plus his family's been at odds with the medical establishment—as your oma would explain if her body hadn't needed to keep creating new forms unto death. We call it cancer. She and I have had that in common.

Growing up here I heard of mother fits, *and this was how my issues were spoken of in town. A local woman suggested a remedy to my aunt, passed down in fact from Oma's own mother. She said to place a heavy thing on my sternum: a bag of flour, a gallon jug, a Bible. Two and a half years after I married Ort, after Bethany's birth, when I was having renewed difficulties, I'd sit you, Agnes, right on my chest while she napped, and you'd stay there for a bit. You played with my hair, and it helped. That's maybe when your father got it in his head that you could keep me sound. And it's true that you, the two of you, have been a remarkable balm. As I hope you can find your ways to being for each other.*

⌄

If my femur was indeed fractured, my blood should be working to heal me, white blood cells fighting any latent infection, stem cells building a callus. Possibly, I'd need surgery, an intramedullary nail to stabilize the bone. I worked with an electrochemist at DDR who'd broken his leg skiing—Wilson Devaney. He gave me the history of the device he'd gotten implanted: pioneered by a German doctor in WWII, the Küntscher nail allowed injured soldiers to return to the front within weeks. Wilson said this with admiration, as if quick-healing Nazis were a good thing.

I wasn't feeling right. I was sweating in a cold house. Maybe I needed antibiotics, Merit might too, crow beaks being notably unsanitary, but at that moment I was unable to pull my thoughts together. If I had, I might've insisted we go to the hospital and the night wouldn't have gone the way it did.

Forgive me. Such speculation aids no one.

I get my family's reticence about medicine. I do. Penicillin—another modern miracle—has a backstory that glorifies the sloppy lab technique of Alexander Fleming. The man took a two-week vacation and came back to find a staphylococcus culture plate he'd left out had grown a mold. This was his brilliance.

The history of science, I will not deny it, is full of lucky men whose mistakes are examined for value, and evil men whose evil is dismissed as immaterial or necessary—or somehow both. Fleming's mold and Küntscher's nails were hailed for giving soldiers, on opposite sides of the battlefield, more chances to die. When bodies are needed as test subject or cannon fodder, science will serve. When bodies are deigned superfluous, science will serve those ends too. But which bodies are needed, which surplus? And what kind of a mind serves science without caring what science serves? I blame Bruce for planting these questions in me. They grow and grow.

I can't blame him for leaving me though—if I were him, I would've left me.

After reading Ruth, I was feeling a little sick. I swung my legs off the couch onto the floor, which was excruciating. I gritted my teeth, stood on one leg, and hopped to the front window. Learning Pop had a good reason not to love me should be comforting. I was not his. This knowledge should fill some gap. It should. A shock, yes, but was it really? I must've known. I felt strangely as if I had, always. Ruth had simply confirmed what should have been obvious. This newfound evidence, this origin story of my alien nature, it should soon begin to heal me. After all, here was the justification for my father's coldness, an explanation for why I had not been loved, a reason why I did not know how to love or be loved now. Why didn't it help? Why wasn't it helping?

As I waited for a psychic scab to start knitting itself, I realized, if I were being brutal and honest (and I was often both), I needed to admit—he'd been no different with Bethany. Ort had been the same father to her as he'd been to me. Biology may be all we are. But try to make it the center of human behavioral theory and you will find nothing explained, all things legitimized.

In some countries, for example, in some centuries—Mina would have been killed at birth or left to die.

I hurt. I felt sicker than any fever warranted because such a choice did not feel beyond me. In another country, another century.

It was still fairly early, but dark out, solstice. Much as I might wish it otherwise, I *was* Pop's. I was his daughter and he was my father—this, because we suffered one another.

That's when I saw lights coming up the drive.

I called out to Bethany. She grabbed the gun and we went out again onto the porch. We were both shaky. Dousing my pain with whiskey wasn't working the way I needed it to and Ruth hadn't helped. Not ever.

A car pulled up beside the house. It was Bruce. Bruce and our daughter. Mina.

Once I saw her, the first time in nearly ten months, I realized she'd changed. While I'd been minding Solo, she hadn't stayed frozen, she'd kept moving. And this made me realize that it was Mina who'd changed everything for me—except me.

The job I left, the bird I built, the mother I hadn't and wasn't: after I gave birth, my North shifted. For nine years I've been stumbling, off balance. Maybe I was unsteady from the beginning, but becoming her mother showed me just how skewed, how far from true level I've been functioning my whole life.

I need her to know that no matter how inadequate I've been—and I have been inadequate—she is the center. I thought I knew that before. I know it now. Is all of this unfair to say? Will she ever read this? Will it make her feel responsible? I don't want that either. Forgive me, I've never known how to do this—love someone the way they deserve to be loved. Least of all a daughter.

Bruce got out first. He circled round to the passenger side. Mina had already flung open the door. I could see she was bigger. He helped her stand and, while still bracing her, he reached into the car and pulled out two elbow crutches.

She's using crutches now.

> What are you doing here, Bruce?
>
> *Your daughter wants you to come for Christmas. We're here to gather you up . . . think of it as an early present. Hi, Bethany.*

I saw him then, eyeing my face, my splinted leg, my sister, the rifle.

When I'd first met this man, he'd been an anti-gun, melt-'em-all type, like his parents and poet-friends. Before I agreed to marry him, I insisted he come out target shooting with me. Told him he wasn't allowed to hate what he didn't know. He thought that was funny, given the tight scope and confines of my upbringing. Well, it turns out he did hate—hated that he loved it. So many things can be like that: guns, whiskey, motherhood. Firing a rifle goes beyond the immediate rush of power. It feels essential, the development of a core competency, like baking bread or learning to read. To deny this is to underestimate a thing we desperately need to understand about each other. We are, all of us, seduced by whatever makes us feel most capable.

What's going on here?

I had no idea how to answer this question. I gestured to my right, toward the tree. Just then, one of the birds flew out and across the front of the porch to pick up gravel from the drive. I flinched, half-expecting it to strafe us, but it didn't. It flew close though, so close Mina's bangs were blown back from her forehead.

She'd cut her bangs.

Bethany spoke then. *You two better come inside.*

∨

The first bits sounded like rain.

We were all in the living room—except for Merit, still asleep upstairs. I told Bruce I wrecked the car, that Bethany had come to help me. He could tell there was more. I wanted to tell him about the crows, and Scylla's body, how they attacked Merit and how Solo hid her away, how he'd meant to protect her, but Mina was sitting right there.

She looked so much older than last winter. Nine is different from eight, from seven and six. She was assessing me. She had every right to. I didn't disclose the day's horror, I couldn't. I needed to convince Bruce to take her back to Baltimore. It wasn't safe here. But I wasn't about to purposefully, needlessly, frighten her.

We heard the noise again, coming from the back of the house. Bethany stood first, and we followed. I leaned my way to the kitchen table where she'd left the bottle. Mina followed me in on her new crutches, nimble, practiced. It hurts—how much I've missed. I dropped into a chair and poured a glass. Bruce glowered the way he sometimes does, when he's biting things back but letting me know he is. There are other times, when he imagines he's stifled all sign of how I've failed them both. But there's no way.

Dust spit out of the fireplace. A few pebbles rolled onto the oak floor. Then, another shower of small sounds. More debris. Quiet. We looked around at each other. Bethany offered an explanation.

> *It's an assembly line. They come out of the tree, one by one, fly over to pick up gravel and head to the roof.*

A clatter of rubble started and stopped. A few-second pause, dirt swirling through the air of the room, and a fourth downpour clattered down the chimney.

> *They did the same thing when Pop made a scarecrow.*
>
> I don't remember any scarecrow.
>
> *He got fed up a few years after you left. Found me throwing the birds some of our winter pig. He put one of Momma's hope-chest dresses on a cross, planted it in the west field, and they answered by dropping stones down the chimney for a week.*

She paused. There was another shower.

> *He was mocking me, he told me, with the cross. They'll stop eventually.*

A louder fragment made its way down the flue. It hit brick and jumped out of the hearth. A white stone. Bruce went over to pick it up. He turned it over in his hand before handing it to me. His eyes asked a question he did not want me to answer out loud.

It was one of the carpal bones of the hand—lunate or capitate. It was small, and there was an articular cartilage cap.

When Mina was a toddler, I studied anatomy so I could correctly apply massage for her spasms. Eventually, she let me know she preferred doing PT with her dad, who was more patient and gentle always. Who didn't push or test her.

Chapter Nine

Another hard shower. More rocks and dirt and dust. I coughed into my elbow. Bruce went and scooped up more disarticulated Scylla. Small bones—phalanges and tarsals and vertebrae, some with bits of flesh still attached, though not much. By this time, I think Mina could tell there was something wrong.

A strange fact: though they aren't our prime scavengers, much of North American carrion removal is facilitated by crows. Their tearing and picking apart makes far more of a carcass available to beetles, maggots, fungi. The bodies are cleared faster. This avian labor is heavily relied upon—but largely unsung. There is precious little praise offered to those who till the dead.

Bruce was looking like he might be sick. I tried to obfuscate, be a mother. Lie.

> Do you want to take Mina out to the computer? Merit was on her art sites earlier, maybe she'd like to see . . .

I didn't sound like me. He got it. He swallowed hard, looked around. Settled on a large mixing bowl on the counter and gently placed the bones he was holding inside it. Washed his hands.

A new sound. The noise now coming from the chimney was different. Wrong. Something coming down that shouldn't be. I pointed to Mina and Bruce moved quickly. He scooped her up and headed into the dining room, telling her it was just more rocks, aren't the crows funny, yes he knows she's perfectly capable of walking, but her mom and aunt need to talk alone. Yes right now.

I hopped over to shut the door behind them. When I turned back, Bethany was holding Scylla's head in her hands.

I assumed.

My sister's face, always pale, was translucent. I don't know why she picked it up, its strips of scalp trailing what was once straw-colored hair, bits of muscle clinging to a jaw—all doubled rows of teeth—the skull pan itself mottled red and pink and brown. Bethany was rigid, holding the thing out in front of her face, her eyes mimicking the large eye sockets, bigger, proportionately, in children. She was pulled up to her full height, maybe five foot two, every muscle tense but not with what I'd call fear.

This was astonishment: a turning of flesh to stone. Or, biblically, salt.

She dropped the head. I cringed. It bounced unceremoniously, leaving parts of itself on the wood: smear and tooth—one of the frontmost baby teeth. Maybe the first one the child had lost.

∨

I found myself getting angry at my sister, which was not a reasonable reaction.

> If they wanted the girl buried, why toss her piece by piece down the fucking chimney?

My tone brought her back to herself. We knew this dance.

> *Well, we didn't bury her, did we? And then your crow brought her back to you.*

> *Not* to me. I don't know why he keeps moving that child's body, but you're the common denominator. You and Merit.

Her lips disappeared when she frowned, just like when she was little.

> *Why, though? Why Merit?*

Merit looks very much like my sister and—despite our different fathers and shades-of-pale—my sister looks like me. I wondered who Scylla had looked like. What books she'd loved or was learning to read. How she'd liked her eggs.

Bethany had gotten quiet too. She went over and passed a hand over the bowl. She took a deep breath before looking at me.

> *Can you ask him?*
>
> What? No.

I shook my head at her, it was absurd. But I knew what she meant.

> Solo, he talks, but . . . not like we remember. What we remember was—it had to be—delusion.
>
> *No.*

Her face. She was not having it.

> Be reasonable, Bethany. Ruth told us she heard them—so we imagined we heard them too.

Bethany sighed. When had she gotten so sure of herself? It must be nice to be so certain of things. Contrafactual things.

> *The crows and the Krahns have lived here together for a long time. They talked to Oma too.*
>
> Oma died long before we were born.
>
> *She was special. More than a dozen years with Pop in this house, Agnes—you don't think I read their books? Oma's too? You haven't scratched the surface, I bet.*
>
> You read Ruth's diary?
>
> *That's the least of it.*

I hadn't considered this possibility. Bethany. I hadn't imagined she might be curious.

> *Pop hated that his mother powwowed. Called her beliefs *guano.* That means . . .*
>
> I know what guano means.
>
> *. . . same as he called mine. Did you know he did four tours in Vietnam? Four. He wasn't expecting to come back, kept signing up*

not to. The crows, though—they choose their own company—you can't enlist. They didn't speak to him.

Why Ruth then?

Because she was sensitive. Like you, me. Like my Merit.

∨

Some Personal Notes on Charms for Daily Living by Hannah Krahn (Oma). ~RK

For the Colic—

Place the child over the knees facing down, rub the back clockwise. Repeat the following: *Ayah, ayah, bay-bee. Tears begone. Jesu-Jesu-Jesu.*

A Salve for after the Switch—*

1 cup rosewater, ½ cup butter, 1 tbsp beeswax, 2 large handfuls of chickweed

*If the switch has broken the skin, remove any stray bark and cleanse with warm water before applying.

Protection Spell for the Childless and Children—

Speak: *Though you have been unchosen for this blessing, God protect you to serve as helpmeet to other women.* Then smash 22 cloves and 3 tablespoons nutmeg into a half-cup almonds, have the woman eat the mixture dry. If she vomits it back up, do not allow her to sit with infants under six months.

When Machines Won't Run

Slather the afflicted person's hands with olive oil. Have them for [3] days and [3] nights avoid all electricity. A hunting cabin will serve. When they emerge, comb their hair forward over their eyes, then cut the longest lock to put in a satchel with a copper coin to keep on their person. *Eligius, Isidore, etc.*

Chapter Nine

To Protect a Grown Child from Harm—

> Speak: *I offer you my Lord his work. I offer you my Lord his mirth. I offer you my Lord his child, the first. Please, my Lord, take one and leave the others to be used in your name.*

∨

Pop left me the house though Bethany lived with him ten years after I'd gone. I spoke with the man not often and rarely visited. After the summer at Salyers I came home a handful of long weekends, Christmases. I'd bring Bethany fuzzy socks and chocolates. Pop looked mad but it was Christmas, what could he say? Him, I'd get something useful: a new hoe or tacklebox. Things I later found he barely used, if at all. I called to talk with Bethany every week or two for years, though we had less and less in common.

Pop didn't believe in much, but he believed in work. *Your sister best contribute*, he said when I was leaving. Starting junior year, she cashiered at a few no-future mom-and-pops that paid her under the table. After high school, she tried waitressing twice, at Hickory Tavern and a place called the Sky Wagon, but was unpracticed at smiling and small talk. A few guys asked her out, no real boyfriends. She wasn't interested in dating, maybe because she'd taken to listening to Bible-thumping radio, all self-hate and hellfire. When she started preaching it to me over the phone, I stopped calling as often. Pop, it made furious.

After I got my copy of the will, I reached out. She said she didn't want the house or land. There wasn't much else. An old farm truck, tractor, plow, some other equipment. Bruce and I put most of it on Craigslist and sent Bethany the cash. The plan was, after he and I fixed up the house and sold it, we'd split the profit with her. It seemed only fair. But when I told her, she said no. Pride inherited from Pop, I guess. I can't see Pastor Derek advising against it.

I don't know why she stayed. I pushed her to try things as much as I could figure a direction to push. When waitressing wasn't it, I said she should cut hair (she did a fair job on Pop's and her own) or start a housecleaning business. Anything to get her out. When I'd nearly given up on her leaving, she met Tim—who shared her love for Jesus Christ, or said he did, which seems like all that's required. I tried to be happy for her. At the wedding, Pop called Tim *a provider*. About Bethany, he said, *She's a strong one*. I'd found this odd, like he was describing a carthorse, but maybe honest. Strength is one of the few things our childhood had to offer.

My little sister was standing in the kitchen of the house in which she'd spent most her life, staring at a child's skull on the floor. How strong was she really? How strong could someone be?

Suffer the little . . . Bethany was shaking her head.

I finished—*children.* Even I know that one.

Bethany nodded.

At church they said the oldest of three.

We have to let the family know. Soon. They're probably imagining the worst.

Bethany's head shot up.

How isn't this the worst?

We stared at each other. I didn't have to say anything more. Solo was a monster, but he wasn't a man. Bethany pursed her lips, huffed out through her nose, looked back down.

Right.

She went to retrieve a dishtowel, then crouched to recover the head, wrap it, and place it tenderly into the bowl before going back to the hearth for more bones: what looked to be a knobby ulna, a tibia, two jagged ribs.

Chapter Nine

I'm embarrassed to say how it felt to be in the kitchen—Bethany and me and the dead child scattered across floor and counter—my sister cleaning up as she always had, taking care of things without complaint, all the horrible things. It wasn't right, but it was very nearly comforting. She knew me, she knew this place. I didn't have to pretend. She knew all I'd started with and where I'd ended up. If she was with me now, there was nothing I could do to lose her.

It was an awkward gift, that knowledge. I didn't want it.

The thing was, I wasn't sure I knew my sister in the same way—in fact, I knew I didn't. How had she become who she'd become? Visits or no, holding babies or no, I'd given up trying to understand her a long time ago. I'd shown up periodically on her doorstep, but for what? There was some thread escaping me, something I'd lost hold of when I'd left her—alone, with Pop.

Bethany, why did he leave me the house?

Her back was to me. She didn't turn, didn't miss a heartbeat. She answered as if she'd been expecting this question.

Because you killed her.

∨

I don't know what I thought Bethany was going to say, but it wasn't that. I slid to the floor, an ugly cry. I was sure Mina would hear me, but Bruce kept her out of the kitchen. Later, I learned the two of them had gone upstairs.

Bethany stood there, at the stove. She put on water.

She let me go on.

I can't remember the last time I'd cried like that, sobbing with my whole body. Not when Ruth died and not with Pop. When Mina was born and I was so afraid she wouldn't make it, before the surgeries to seal her spine, I didn't cry. But her dad did.

Bruce was so worried, she was too beautiful he said that's why he worried, that our baby was maybe too beautiful to live—a garbage thought only a poet would have.

I had a job, and it was to keep her alive if I could. To hold her against me as instructed, skin to skin, to breastfeed her, though I never got good at it, to change and soothe and bathe her. I'd fucked up but it didn't matter. Once Mina was born, that was my job, and I did it until it was my job to go back to work, pumping breastmilk in DDR's breakroom (though I was never good at it) so Bruce could keep her alive, because that was his job now.

I had three months with her, most of it in the NICU with a team of nurses who knew her needs better than I did—Val and Deedee and Grace—and that was it. Later, when I'd come home from the lab, Bruce would hand her over and I wouldn't know what to do, what to say or sing.

Ruth's songs seemed to mutate on my tongue. I hadn't learnt them well enough, and I couldn't learn my daughter. When I admitted this to Bruce, he downloaded an album of Irish lullabies. Ruth had sung us "Tora Lora Lora" and "Shoo La Rue." I'd thought the nonsense hers, but the nonsense was in the originals. I tried to sing them. But Mina didn't like it when I sang—only Bruce's voice could stop her crying.

> *Pop wanted you to come back.*
>
> Why?
>
> *To live here, without her. Like we did.*

The house was a punishment . . . of course it was.

> Did he think she would get better? How much pain did he want her to have?

He loved her, Agnes.

We were his children.

I sounded like a child. The water was boiling. Bethany turned it off, put teabags in two mugs. I was still on the floor.

He gave us her days, he had her nights. When I told him what we'd done—he said we stole from him, and not grain or ham. Hours, days, weeks.

She poured out the steaming water, then put the kettle back on the stove, a different burner.

It's what she wanted.

I said that, but did I know? I know I didn't want to carry it alone. I know there was no way to apologize. I had Bethany stir the lime into Ruth's cup, had her take it to Ruth, help Ruth sip it down. I told her the crows said to. When you ask someone to go against themselves like that, whatever love survives between you gets tainted. It was me, I was the poison.

What could've possessed you to tell him?

I shouldn't have said it that way. Bethany squinted into one of the mugs. She lifted out the bag and laid it on the old linoleum. Where it would stain.

*Tim's old-fashioned. Came to ask Pop for my hand, and Pop said . . . he said he didn't know why he'd want it . . . that Jesus had already *fucked* me good.*

She pushed the word out of her mouth like a moth that'd flown in. Wet and wrong.

*That night, at supper, after Tim was gone I said to him, to Pop—at least *I* wasn't so nuts the crows in my head had me killed.*

She brought the mug to her chapped lips. The two of us take our tea without sugar because we aren't weak, we don't need any bullshit sweetener. You have tea because you want tea.

But you don't think they were in her head.

She looked at me like I was an idiot.

I was trying to hurt him. He knew Ruth heard them, Oma too. But that was his whole religion . . . not believing.

I needed to stop underestimating my sister.

If it's not in our heads, what is it?

She was prepared for this.

They're our Gethsemane.

And just when she was sounding sane, out came the Jesus shit. Again.

No one else hears them, Bethany. If we hear them, we're as unfit as she was.

She laughed at me, shook her head.

You think we were a mistake? Agnes, God doesn't make mistakes.

Hadn't we been raised in the same house? How had she not learned to think for herself? Her mind was sharp—why did she insist on dulling it with wall-plaque platitudes?

There's a dead girl, here, in this room. (I pointed to the bowl.) It's tragic, yes, but there's no god involved. No grand plan, Bethany, just nature and run-of-the-mill dysfunction.

They told me to kill him.

She was serious.

What?

After you left they told me how to do it—a shallow pit, the tractor. But I resisted and God is why. I have been absolved. You failed your test, not me.

She was fucking crazy. My sister had gone over the edge—it was in our genes after all. Still . . . it was true I'd failed.

I know a thousand ways to fail.

Gently, she put down her own cup and reached to the bowl. She laid her fingertips on top of Scylla's skull, like bread rising under the dishtowel, one with a black tulip design I'd picked out at Zimmer's.

*Your crow killed this poor baby, that monster *you* made because of who *you* are. You need to fix this.*

What I saw in my sister's face wasn't anger or illness. She was pleading with me to red up my house, to clean the mess I'd made, but to do it right this time. To carry what I'd insisted on carrying—and not just up to the porch—but all the way inside.

Chapter Ten

A SOLITUDE OF CROWS

∨

Ness, Bethany—you have to come see this—

Sound has always carried strangely in this house, stealing in and out of rooms like an intruder, one desperate enough to enter its dry-rotted husk. Bethany helped me onto my good foot and into the dining room. Bruce was at the top of the stairs looking down, Merit at his side. Our raised voices must've brought on a nightmare—he told us she'd cried out. Pretty sure the crows had some role in that, but I didn't mention it.

He'd taken Mina with him to wake her cousin from a bad dream. Merit stood there, curls askew, squinting down at her mother and me, holding Bruce's hand though she didn't know him. He's infuriatingly good with small people. I didn't see Mina.

We started up. Bethany was quicker, soon standing behind her daughter, waiting on me. I had to go one step at a time, leaning heavily on the banister. She smoothed out some of Merit's tangles, then kissed the crown of her head. Ruth had done that—kissed our heads, smelled them. She'd kept a pitcher of infused well water by the tub for rinsing, lavender or rosemary or mint. Back when she was bathing us—before it was the other way around—she'd extol us with their various properties: comfort, vigor, clarity. Botanical drivel.

Chapter Ten

Once I got up the first flight, Bruce pointed to the narrow staircase curving up to the attic.

While I was calming this one, Mina went exploring.

The man had clearly let her. I'd never taken Mina up to the attic, it wasn't a place for children. Just junk up there, I told her, plus the stairs were no good. And they weren't: too-thin triangles, like overlaid blades, built for no feet I'd ever seen, built for falling. She'd asked and I'd said no. Now that she was back in this place and her father distracted, up she went. Mina has always hated nos, can'ts, don'ts. Since infancy, she's regarded us like we're the limited ones, me especially. It's maddening.

Again I was last up, and there she was—proudly displaying her find.

I thought it was a Jackson Pollock knockoff at first, maybe one of hers, because of the colors, but it wasn't just spatter, and I soon realized the work predated our time together in this house. The canvas stood half-pulled out from behind an access panel, yellow insulation erupting from the crawl space. The yellow cloud piled up around Mina's ankles. She looked smug as a cat, some half-dead thing in its clutch. I looked closer.

Two pale faces, like oblong moons. Sleeping—lilac-lidded.
Both faces veiny beneath milky skin. A hand resting
across green: a white spider in the grass.

She pointed to another on the ground a few feet away. She nodded at Merit, who wrested free from her mother to join her. *Can you pick it up?* Mina asked the younger girl. It was nearly as big as she was, but Merit managed, smiling wide, thrilled to be trusted with a matter of obvious consequence. The stunned quiet of adults told her as much.

Two ovals shrouded in masses of dark and light threads.
Faces behind filament, turned from one another.
All colors muted, cloudy bottle.

And then I noticed the path. Three more paintings on the floor leading from the east side of the attic to the south. The final one Mina had somehow managed to drag into the middle of Ruth's carpet. I made my way over.

A closeup of skin: one cheekbone beneath
spreading lashes, the other constellated with freckles.
A summer painting, starlit.

Bruce followed, pointing out the other wall panels as he walked over. *There could be more, these colors are . . .* He couldn't come up with a word. I looked at Bethany standing back at the top of the stairs. She bit her bottom lip, deciding something.

Pop showed me one once . . . way back. I'd forgotten. Said he was going to pile all her work under the locust and burn it. I put it out of my mind. If he was going to destroy what was left of her, I wasn't about to let myself care.

The house I'd grown up in was packed foundation to shingle with withholding—but Mina somehow knew where to look.

You just . . . found them?

There were all these doors.

She tapped one with her crutch. Each access panel had a circular metal pull, inset low, about a foot from the ground. *Crawl*, Mina told me in the dream, *crawl.*

But *how* did you?

She looked at me with disgust. Pity.

*I can *do* lots of things.*

I heard Halmoni's voice when she said that, scolding me, but it didn't matter. The way Mina looked—so angry and so sad at me. Can a person be sad *at* someone? I think yes because she was that, I felt it. She maneuvered the tip of a crutch through the nearest pull and yanked. I made out three more canvases stacked against each other. She peered into the dark space. *She tried so hard, I think*, she searched for the words, *to make you how she wanted you to be*. It was a strange way to see Ruth's paintings. It was not how I saw them.

She wanted us asleep?

Mina crinkled her face. *No.*

Then she rolled her eyes like any preteen dealing with any clueless mother. How I wish that could've been us. But my failures went deeper.

Together.

Then her eyes softened, and she pointed her crutch along the path of paintings.

She never showed you these?

She did not.

But they're so beautiful.

Mina peered into the crawlspace then, her face unfolding like she suddenly understood something. All this time, I wonder, has she thought me a miser? Did my daughter think I've been keeping the best parts of myself from her on purpose?

That's not what's wrong with me. I don't have best parts. I wish I did. I don't have Ruth's beauty. Or her light. I don't see the things she saw, not how she saw them. I can't laugh the way she did, I never could, not even when I was with her. Before the cancer. I was always waiting for her good days to go dark, and that's how I missed them. I don't think there's any of her in me—and I don't know why there isn't.

I loved her. But I did it terribly.

All those Polaroids. Do you remember?

Bethany was talking.

> *Boxes and boxes. Pop had them shredded because of all the time I spent looking. He said *Memory is gluttony.* Mine was, at least. But he kept these—all to himself. He lived up here with them. With her. He never really wanted to share her with us.*

I wonder, had Pop ever been whole? Maybe he'd come back from the war without some crucial piece. It might've been taken from him. That, or lost. Could he have given it away? Sold it? Shot it? It's possible, of course, that he never had it to begin with. I feel like that can happen.

⌄

Letter, cont.

> . . .
>
> *The day you were born, Mina, I thought I was miscarrying. It isn't an excuse, it's the truth. It was too early, and I still didn't believe I could be a mother. I hadn't been grown on the proper substrate.*
>
> *Here's what I remember.*
>
> *I came home to an empty house. All day long I'd been cramping, my ankles were swollen, the walk home nearly had me vomiting. It was June, the humidity rising in wet waves from the asphalt. I was sweating rivulets. I took the way home that had the most trees, a recently planted block of Bradford pears—quick growers found on the berms of all the city's gentrifying pockets. I just wanted to breathe. I tried the doorknob before I remembered your dad was gone for the night.*
>
> *He'd taken the Megabus to New York for a book launch in Brooklyn—a grad school buddy. He was staying over. He didn't ask me to go anymore, even when they were in town. This one was going to be insufferable. Jace wasn't talented, what-he-was was a good-*

looking guy with family money who lived in the right city and ran a reading series. Philly was the wrong city but your father swore he'd never leave.

Is Baltimore good, Mina? Your grandparents—doting as ever?

Your father was not there when I doubled over. He was not there when I decided to face your death alone. Not there when, in the bathtub of our apartment, you burst out of me not-quite-passed-out-drunk only because contractions don't really let you do that. The world was a sauna, the windows were open, and my wailing prompted our neighbor to call for an ambulance. It took them some time to show up, because Kensington, but eventually the EMTs found us. You and me and the red river that led from the tub out into the hallway and poured down the narrow stairs of the two-story rental your dad wasn't supposed to have painted. A river murky as the Schuylkill.

That is your birth story. As complete as I can make it.

So it was indeed my alcohol-induced stupor that kept me from distinguishing early labor from miscarriage and from getting us to a hospital. Oxygen deprivation may have caused your palsy. The doctors said we can't know for sure.

*The spina bifida occurred earlier, the result of me exposing you to toxins in utero. That part you know about. I was technically at fault, but it served DDR's interests to have me sign an NDA. Transparency is not part of their worldview. The civil suit was settled in our favor despite all complications—your grandparents are very good lawyers, as I'm sure they've told you. They don't approve of me, and why should they? Halmoni once called me a too-bright rube. Your dad repeated it often. He finds the term *amusingly musical*—a phrase he also likes.*

Beyond my failings, please remember it was poetry that kept your father from both of us on that day. Remember that when he recites it to you.

No, I'm wrong. Don't. Poetry can be beautiful stuff. Useless beautiful stuff.

⌄

A crow raised one
hell of a hell
—all knowns

unsaid, each birth
a still, all stone
brimming with none.

~BN

⌄

Bruce helped me lift more paintings out into the space. All the same subject: me and Bethany. We were centered in some, obscured or fragmented in others. Only the colors of our childhood quilts assured me this was us, woven into the landscape of Ruth's insomnia. Here was the record of my mother's disintegration—a piecework of sleeping daughters, stitched together with inadequate threads of love.

Mina and Merit were poring over them too, pointing out which they thought was mother, which aunt, guessing at a chronology, asking us why we hadn't had our own beds. This was a problem for both of them. Merit may have little she considers her own, but a mattress, yes—the lower bunk because Honor's got the top. *My bed's sort of like a top bunk*, Mina told her, *but on the ground . . . it's got rails.* She was warming to her, this new cousin of hers.

He couldn't do it, Bethany was muttering, *not melt our faces.*

She was right. Ruth had fixed them in place. Pop didn't believe, but he was stuck. His love for her meant he couldn't raze her magic. Her talent, what she felt for us, saw in us, her illnesses, the cancer and the other one—it was all here. The whole unholy spectrum of it.

A window broke.

On the far side of the attic, glass flew into the room and with it, a crow, lighting on Pop's bare cot and shaking his feathers like an old man tapping rain from an umbrella. He settled, then eyed us, as if to decide on the subject of the necessary lecture or sermon. After our initial shock, Bethany took it upon herself, the ridding. She ran at him, shouting, *Git. Git now!*

The bird flew out and we heard the ones below, suddenly loud, an overlapping roll call of chatter and rumor. We'd been delivered a directive it seemed, and we heeded it, hurrying two floors down. Bethany, I knew, would want the rifle.

Merit reached the ground floor before any of us.

We descended, one after another: Bethany following Merit, then Mina and Bruce, then me—giving up any pretense of uprightness and thumping painfully down on my ass. What we saw when we reached the bottom of the stairs, I find difficult to describe. I can sketch an outline, but I can't fill in how it felt. How it took over the room, the night. Everything. It was too much to face, what I'd done.

There he is—

Merit was in the center of the living room, curls shaking, arm stretched towards the window.

Right there. She sounded not scared . . . elated.

Under a cloud backlit by the moon, the greenhouse was a ghost of glass and Solo atop it in freakish weathervane. The image could've been ripped straight out of a book on gothic terror or stoicism:

an illustration of the misguided desire to control nature—that unruly self.

To insulate chosen flora against weather, to remove them from their ecosystems, to transplant them into quarters, close but segmented, to quarantine them from outside interaction—a greenhouse serves the same purposes as a laboratory. No matter what it's meant to grow, a lab works on principles of limitation and elimination, defined by what it excludes. Like the barn where I kept Solo. Like the house where I was kept.

Isolation is a tool of analysis. It is not a state to maintain indefinitely.

Pop and Opa assembled this building for Ruth when I was an infant, just weeks before Opa's death. His father had lived to work, Ruth wanted to grow indigo for her own dyes, Pop wanted his new wife happy. Her bluehouse was a rigid, gable-style, ten-by-sixteen-foot structure with a galvanized steel frame now rusting. It was not built to withstand the weight of much more than the bit of snow that for a few weeks a year clung to its glass-paneled roof, sloped more steeply than either house or barn. It wasn't large, but Solo's silhouette turned it into a toy. I braced myself, waiting for the report of glass buckling, breaking under the strain of the bird, but it didn't come. Bethany let go of Merit's shoulders and started walking toward the front door. I heard her whisper, *No, you don't.*

At that moment, Merit bolted in the opposite direction. She took off like a sprinter through the kitchen and out through the mudroom barefoot, wearing only my thin t-shirt and leggings. Bethany pivoted to run after her. Bruce got up, set Mina on the couch, and told her to stay there. She was not happy—at all. She looked to me, but I held up my hand, seconding him despite myself, signaling for her to wait before heading out after them. I followed slowly, hindered by my leg. The trip to the attic and back had rendered it less than stable.

By the time I'd reached the kitchen garden, the bird was coming off the greenhouse, his impossibly dark wings spread beyond its walls.

Chapter Ten

The moon behind him made Solo's anatomy inscrutable. A blackout. There was no form, just pitch and force, energy quivering in the air above us. He was huge. Horrible. Through the ends of his extended wings I saw the sky, primary feathers opening wide as he repurposed the physics of lift to slow his descent. He retracted his wings only as he set down on the ground.

Merit was there standing below him, a few feet in front of him in the snow, expectant, not defiant, a frost-struck marigold, unflappable and shivering.

He cawed and she nodded.

He cawed, and she spoke. She commanded in a voice older than her years, *Bring me.*

A few feet behind her daughter, Bethany was on her knees pleading for her to come back into the house. Bruce was out front—I first heard, then turned to see him tramping toward us through unbroken snow with the gun. He must've noticed Bethany starting for it and nabbed it from beside the front door. I made my way along the side of the house to meet him at the gate. Despite my leg, I got to it first and opened the latch. I turned back.

It took a few seconds for me to piece together what I was looking at, the reason why my sister hadn't moved forward to grab her daughter.

Solo was on one foot. His other was lifted and outstretched above Merit, its talons like scythes. Three curved over and the fourth, the hallux beneath, poised to snap shut in under-blade. Bethany was down in the snow reaching to her child, Bruce was aiming a rifle he had no business holding, and Merit was intent on the crow who looked inclined to eviscerate her—as he had Scylla.

The world was frozen like that for me, in Polaroid.

It was Merit who rent the stillness. She lifted her small hand, reaching out to touch the tip of a talon as long as her torso. Two figures in a medieval etching of some lost virtue—*insight* or *communion*. Then she drew back her hand.

I watched Solo turn the massive claw sideways. He widened it and shifted it forward almost mechanically, to grasp the child around her waist. But instead of snatching her up as I'd watched him do with cats and rabbits and once an injured possum I'd brought in from the field, he suddenly opened his wings and lifted, skimming over both Merit and Bethany, only to alight closer to the house.

There, lit by the bulb above the mudroom door, Mina emerged.

My Mina.

His talons closed around her like a vice.

He slung her sideways and her crutches fell away. Her legs hung limp. She was so still—too shocked or smart to fight—and something broke in me.

Bethany had run to Merit. They were both closer to the greenhouse than to the bird, holding one another, clasped. I hated them.

Then the two of them began to howl—crying out for Mina? For something. The sound sliced through the space between us, strange and familiar. Without at first realizing it, I joined them. My ribs rang in pain as I let out air from the base of my lungs. Our cries were raw and desperate, but mine was something else. It was inhuman.

Beside me, I felt Bruce's whole body go rigid as he took aim. I stopped wailing—there was no time. The man did not know how to shoot, not after a single day at the range more than a decade ago. If he managed to hit anything, it might've been our daughter. I reached across him, grabbed the barrel of the gun, yanked hard. He wasn't expecting that. He let it drop. I felt the weight of Ort's rifle, the gun I'd learned to fire when I was eleven, and swung it into me. I leaned back, my useless leg and hip pressed up against the fence post, my other leg planted like a pike. I pulled the butt up to my shoulder.

A few yards beyond its sights, the flight I'd promised Mina, built for her, bred for her, had contorted into this winged blackness. This nightmare crow.

Solo crouched, ready to take off from one leg. Mina was horizontal, her paintbrush hair trailing in the snow as an immense bird body loomed above her. If he collapsed, she'd be caught beneath. I had to time my shot, get him as he was propelling forward off the ground so that when he dropped her, she'd fall behind. Instinctively I knew this, even as Bruce yelled, *Ness goddammit shoot*, even as Merit's cry-turned-whimper twanged in some taut place below my diaphragm. I steadied myself. I pulled my elbow toward my rib, and I reached my left hand along the forestock—thumb on the barrel, chin down and in, like Pop taught me.

Solo extended his body, ready to push off. Bethany was in the snow on top of Merit, avoiding the scene, turned away from what he might have done to her child. She, too, had stopped screaming. And in the space where our voices had been . . . nothing. So much dropped away in that long moment. Sound, pain, thought.

I felt clear. As if I were made of vision—my entire body concentrated on the bird. Aimed at. Killing him.

Solo pressed his weight through the single, unencumbered leg normally accordioned under him. Then, in an instant, both legs were fully stretched behind, and Mina—she was gripped above the ground beneath his fanning tail feathers. I felt my finger on the trigger, my sight leading just in front of Solo's breast, where his head was, its dead eye. I took a breath deep into my belly, and . . .

I didn't.

Oh Mina.

I couldn't.

He rose up out of the garden, pumping his wings heavily. And I watched. I watched him climb the air until he was maybe three stories up, above the house. He was still clutching Mina. Too high anymore to chance it. I dropped the gun and looked to Bruce. His face was knotted. Anguish? No. Contempt. He let out a guttural moan and it triggered something in me I hadn't known was there.

I let go another sound, a screech into the dry air.

This one was a call.

The first bird hit Solo's wing, and he faltered.

From behind me, over the top of the house, they erupted like a volley of bats. They rewrote the sky—now a field of black wheat, rustling under their wings. Another black bird shot up from the shadow, targeting the much larger crow.

And then another.

Solo pulled up into himself, beating his wings, pounding the air in an attempt to free himself to turn. But they moved in coordinated attack, a salvo of beaks and bodies, one after another shooting out from the cloud that moved over the house, bulleting into Solo from below. He still held her, he was pulling her up into him. In protection.

One went for his neck. Solo's head wrenched. He convulsed in momentary seizure, contracting in pain I could feel. He somehow managed to open his wings, to right himself. But, in doing so, he dropped Mina.

It was a near forty-foot plummet into the hard snow below. Her body landed a few yards beyond the northern edge of the kitchen garden.

Bruce sprang towards her. He raced across beds the two of them had planted together—asleep now under the snow—vaulted over the wire mesh and dropped down next to her, crumpled. Mina, unmoving.

Overhead, the birds shrieked their displeasure. Solo swiped at them with his talons. He caught a small soldier in the battering of a wing. That crow, stunned, fell. And so it went: the same attacks repeated, the same defense. Several smaller birds rained down into the garden. A few recovered and quickly returned to the air, others staggered across the ground, others did not stir. The riotous echo harsh. Punitive.

Bethany was cradling Merit. Bruce had pulled Mina onto his lap. He started caressing her face.

I was across the garden. Me, unmoving.

Suspended on invisible strands like prey on a web, I felt only the predatory vibrations from approaching darkness—it came from all sides, from decades ago, from the moments ahead. A mass of crows swirled above me, a vortex united to take down this mutant, their-own-not-their-own. Solo. I heard rage, a type of wrath reserved for the stray, the one who wanders, who reveals the order as false. Ruth was such a one. Maybe Pop, too, refusing to be his parents' conduit into the future. Denying us Opa's discipline, Oma's beliefs, their joint practice of raising and slaughtering. He had not wanted his daughters to play at god, making and taking life as they saw fit.

I'd found my way to it anyway.

I shook myself loose and picked the gun up off the ground. To get to Mina and Bruce, I had to pass under the chaos. They were coming at Solo in clusters now, ants meeting an intruder, willing to sacrifice any number of selves in their collective effort. There were hundreds. Maybe thousands. The sky was too dark to count, and it was starting to snow.

Solo had to die. I knew this. I'd maybe known this for a long time.

He twisted, contorting his body, clawing at the onslaught, and a cadre of arrowing birds, sensing vulnerability, shot out from the group to pummel his underside, their combined force pushing him further from the house. A last strike.

His wings pulled in and Solo fell hard. Bethany saw it coming and yanked Merit away, toward the house. When his spine hit the corner of the greenhouse, my back seized. I jabbed the rifle into the ground to steady myself. I watched the building collapse frame-by-frame inward, the impact a quake I felt in my eardrums. Panes burst, steel beams folded in and disappeared beneath his black. And then he was pulled under: an ice sculpture crashing through the melting surface of a lake in a thicket of mirroring shards. For an instant, I saw all the other birds among the falling flakes. A kaleidoscope, Solo at the center.

Every bird was one bird, and the one—all.

Their hatred for him did not keep them from being him. What was he but their worst selves writ large? His intellect and his cruelty, indexes of one another. He was a god, created as gods are, through collective imagination, investment, distortion. They could not deny him. And because they could not, they needed to end him.

The structures built to protect the self from recognizing itself are fragile and monstrous.

Briefly, in a flash like summer lightning, I saw the horror clearly.

Solo was my own crow.

∨

After that everything is fragments.

Chapter Ten

∨

Her father carried Mina inside. He shouldn't have moved her at all, but Bruce wasn't thinking straight. We knew not to call an ambulance. Not with pieces of Scylla there in the kitchen. Not with Bruce, Black. Mina was breathing, shallowly.

∨

He laid her on the couch. Bethany and Merit stood above her. They put hands on her chest and stomach. Bethany took a deep breath then and began chanting. After a round, Merit joined her. Bruce stood beside, protective and wary, but he didn't stop them.

∨

*Lord Jesus, thy wounds so red will guard me against death. Dullix, ix, ux. Yea, you can't come over Pontio; Pontio is above Pilato. Lord Jesus, thy wounds so red will guard me against death. Dullix, ix, ux. Yea, you can't come over Pontio; Pontio is above Pilato. Lord Jesus, thy wounds so red will guard me against death. Dullix, ix, ux. Yea, you can't come over Pontio; Pontio is above Pilato.**

∨

I stood on one leg at the edge of the kitchen, watching this sideshow. Regretting every single thing I'd ever done, every thing I'd failed to do. The lists were long.

∨

Is it awful if I say I wanted their prattling to work, that I was willing to believe anything just to have Mina open her eyes? Or is it more awful to admit I had not one such thought, that I was furious that they could take comfort in this filth?

∨

It felt to me like filth.

∨

I had nothing to offer. I held the gun, had used it as a walking stick to get inside the house, this clapboard block of hell. By this time your father—in shock—had dropped to the floor beside Mina and was massaging her hand and wrist. When my sister and her daughter finished their litany, he started speaking softly to Mina, begging her to wake up, please, going on about goddamned Christmas, asking what she wanted, describing the snow outside which was falling in fat, fat flakes.

∨

But Mina, she is also my child. None of this crap woke her.

∨

Those few minutes stretched taut, ready to snap. I finally spoke. I said—We need to get Mina to the hospital. Bethany drove.

* From *A Long Lost Friend.*

Chapter Ten

DEC26

Mina—

I write in the lobby. It's decorated with fake greens, red bulbs, white lights—it couldn't be more generic. I lie. It's lovely, actually. I keep refusing to have my leg looked at. I don't think it's broken, don't care if it is. We've been here since we brought you, only going back to the house for showers and brief bouts of sleep. We trade on and off. Your father isn't really speaking to me, but he also won't let his parents come. A small kindness. He's exhausted. I think I'm supposed to be comforting him, but I seem incapable of that small humanity.

You have fifteen separate fractures, some internal bleeding, swelling of the brain. We told the doctors you fell from the barn loft, that you'd climbed up there against our wishes. Partial truths make for more believable lies, and the weight training you've done these past months has made you strong.

Still, social services pulled me aside twice. Ms. Garza is maybe a decade younger than me but tired, scolding, and skeptical in her pencil skirt, clicking notes into her iPad. I'm not looking pretty, but Bethany says they won't push too hard because *We take religious liberty seriously around here.* Your aunt has come in every day to check on you . . . and me. I didn't ask her how exactly she thinks the domestic abuse they assume equates with freedom. It's not the time. Anyway, I can be intimidating when I need to be: woman scientist, parents-in-law lawyers on speed dial, a question of my husband's civil rights, etc. Your father, he deserves none of this. But the idea that he's responsible for our injuries? It'd be beyond laughable if I didn't see him seeing it in their faces.

You haven't had to be intubated. He takes it as a hopeful sign—that you're still breathing on your own. I am less sure you'll choose to stay with us.

I've begun thinking of it as that—your choice.

Yesterday was Christmas. I slept from 2 to 6 a.m., then woke and went down to the kitchen. I half-expected Scylla to be there on the counter. She wasn't. Three days ago, your dad and I collected as much of her as we could find and in the dead of night left her at a fire station with no cameras. It's not good enough, but it was the course of action we'd agreed upon.

After I brewed, spiked, and drank my coffee, I made my way outside. Slowly. My leg may not be broken, but it's not right. Your dad and I haven't yet discussed what to do with Solo. A fire, probably. Like the one Rainbow Crow ferried to earth to make winter survivable. Remember? As if surviving is ever enough.

The snow was impossibly bright. Prisms everywhere. The world shone—glass made glitter, ground finer than pain. I don't know how it can be that way. I don't know why beauty is allowed to exist here, of all places. It does—that's all.

I made my way through the kitchen garden, and I counted.

> Eleven dead crows.
>
> One dead child. Poor, undone Scylla.
>
> Two wounded daughters—Merit awake, you sleeping.
>
> And two daughter-mothers, halves of a fractured moon long since gone dark.

I got to the ruins and didn't immediately see Solo. It took some time for my eyes to adjust to the glare off the broken panes. When they did, I realized he wasn't there. There was some blood pooled, there was a trail.

Chapter Ten

I followed it down the slope, between the pond and pen, out past the trees into the north field. It makes no sense, Mina, I know, but as I wandered into the snow between weeds and remnants of wild corn, I kept thinking I was Dorothy.

Dorothy from *The Wizard of Oz.*

You and I watched it together. Your dad was at a reading. He thought it might be too grisly for you—this was back in Philly, you were maybe five, I didn't think so. You had sparkly sneakers I thought ridiculous (why did you need sneakers?) but you loved beyond reason. I'd seen the film once before, at a drive-in Ruth had taken us to, also against our father's wishes because faerie tales are dangerous. They make you think things can happen that can't happen.

You adored it.

You loved everything about the film, but you were a strange little bird and you loved the flying monkeys best. I asked you if you wanted one. No. You wanted to *be* one. A few months later we all watched *The Wiz* together—you, me, and your dad—and you loved that too, all except for Evilene's henchmen. They were scary but that wasn't what bothered you. You saw their motorcycles and burst into tears, inconsolable. You were devastated. *Why*, you asked me, *did these ones ride on wheels and not the sky?*

The path of blood through stalks in the morning light: it was as if all Oz's colors had been mixed up. Dorothy's dress was cornflower blue—here the sky was. Her shoes were ruby, but red was the river I seem to have crossed into nowhere. I saw the yellow brick road in dead foliage beside the path, gold unspun . . . turned back to straw.

And then it started to snow. Peacefully, blissfully. Exactly like in the 1939 movie, when they see the Emerald City from the sleepy poppy field: green sparkling in the distance, like spring, a next place, but so very far away. Too far. I reached the end of the blood trail, found a large indentation where Solo had no doubt lain down to die.

And a few feet beyond that, him. My own crow.

For uncountable seconds, all color was sucked from the world. There was only the bird and the snow and the still, cold air. And then, slowly, bit by bit, it crept back in and what had threatened to become black-and-white—wasn't.

He was dead, but there was still blue.

Blue, in his wings.

⌄

In the beginning
was the fear and
the fear was

with love
and the fear was love.
Q: What is loss

if not an end to fear
without an end
to love?

A: Loss is crows.

~BN

∨

WINR (online)

Carston (44) and Laynie (25) Durfee were arrested Friday evening, police reported.

The married couple has been charged with multiple felony offenses, including child endangerment, assault, and murder.

The Durfees are accused of the continuing physical abuse of their two younger children and of incurring, through similar abuse, the death of an older daughter whose partial remains were recovered by the authorities two days before Christmas.

It appears that the Durfees were in Letort evading an investigation initiated by the Washington DC CFSA (Child and Family Services Agency). We will report more as further information comes to light.

We are relieved to relate that the two remaining children have been taken into protective custody and are no longer in imminent danger. We would like to thank the public for their help in the search for the missing girl, Scylla, whose bones provided the forensic information which ultimately led to these arrests, Lancaster police said on their CrimeWatch page.

The police are asking the party who delivered the girl's incomplete skeleton to the Blue Rock Fire Rescue Station to please step forward. Questions remain.

THE END

ACKNOWLEDGMENTS

In deep appreciation of Siân Griffiths; may she never rue the day. For their beyond generous readings: Ann Kaschock, Taryn Kaschock Russell, Sarah Yake, Brandon Haffner, Emma Burcart, Mikey Rioux, Addie Tsai, Danielle Pafunda, Hawken Pafunda, and the stellar Jennifer Stanford. Thank you also, Ted Fristrom and Nino Gambashidze. To so many teachers of so many types: Sarah Jane Duax, Amy Brown, Patrick Lawler, Brooks Haxton, Reginald McKnight, Mary Oliveira, and the corner-charm-repeating Rachel Wenrick. Finally, to the hearts that live outside my body: Danny, Simon, Bishop, and Koen.

KIRSTEN KASCHOCK has earned degrees from Yale University, University of Iowa, Syracuse University, University of Georgia, and Temple University. A Pew Fellow in the Arts and Summer Literary Seminars grand prize winner, Kirsten is the author of multiple poetry collections, including *Unfathoms*, *A Beautiful Name for a Girl*, *The Dottery*, *Confessional Science-fiction: A Primer*, *Explain This Corpse*, *AutoPortrait (as flotsam)* forthcoming, and a debut speculative novel—*Sleight*. She has taught writing at several schools including Drexel University, St. Lawrence University, and Maryland Institute College of Art (MICA).

This volume is the thirty-first recipient of the Juniper Prize for Fiction, established in 2004 by the University of Massachusetts Press in collaboration with the UMass Amherst MFA Program for Poets and Writers, to be presented annually for an outstanding work of literary fiction. Like its sister award, the Juniper Prize for Poetry established in 1976, the prize is named in honor of Robert Francis (1901–1987), who lived for many years at Fort Juniper, Amherst, Massachusetts.

www.ingramcontent.com/pod-product-compliance
Lightning Source LLC
LaVergne TN
LVHW091128080826
845145LV00008B/2081

* 9 7 8 1 6 2 5 3 4 9 2 5 5 *